HONEYMOON'S OVER

Clint fired again and the four men, caught in the cross-fire somehow, all hit the floor, dead. When they weren't blocking the doorway he saw a man in the other room holding a gun. He held his fire, because the man seemed to have helped him.

"What the—" he said, then saw the man turn his gun toward the bed. "No!" he shouted, but he was too late. The man fired once and Jane Hutchinson hit the floor, also dead. She was lying half on and half off the bed, her legs on it, her butt in the air.

"Jesus," Clint said. "What the hell did you do that for?"

The man entered the room, approached the bed, leaned over, and took a small .32-caliber pistol from the dead woman's hand.

THE GUNSMITH

279

DEATH IN DENVER

J. R. ROBERTS

JOVE BOOKS, NEW YORK

THE BERKLEY PUBLISHING GROUP
Published by the Penguin Group
Penguin Group (USA) Inc.
375 Hudson Street, New York, New York 10014, USA
Penguin Group (Canada), 10 Alcorn Avenue, Toronto, Ontario M4V 3B2, Canada
(a division of Pearson Penguin Canada Inc.)
Penguin Books Ltd., 80 Strand, London WC2R 0RL, England
Penguin Group Ireland, 25 St. Stephen's Green, Dublin 2, Ireland (a division of Penguin Books Ltd.)
Penguin Group (Australia), 250 Camberwell Road, Camberwell, Victoria 3124, Australia
(a division of Pearson Australia Group Pty. Ltd.)
Penguin Books India Pvt. Ltd., 11 Community Centre, Panchsheel Park, New Delhi—110 017, India
Penguin Group (NZ), Cnr. Airborne and Rosedale Roads, Albany, Auckland 1310, New Zealand
(a division of Pearson New Zealand Ltd.)
Penguin Books (South Africa) (Pty.) Ltd., 24 Sturdee Avenue, Rosebank, Johannesburg 2196, South
Africa

Penguin Books Ltd., Registered Offices: 80 Strand, London WC2R 0RL, England

This is a work of fiction. Names, characters, places, and incidents either are the product of the author's imagination or are used fictitiously, and any resemblance to actual persons, living or dead, business establishments, events, or locales is entirely coincidental.

DEATH IN DENVER

A Jove Book / published by arrangement with the author

PRINTING HISTORY
Jove edition / March 2005

Copyright © 2005 by Robert J. Randisi.

ISBN: 0-515-13901-7

JOVE®
Jove Books are published by The Berkley Publishing Group,
a division of Penguin Group (USA) Inc.
375 Hudson Street, New York, New York 10014.
JOVE is a registered trademark of Penguin Group (USA) Inc.
The "J" design is a trademark belonging to Penguin Group (USA) Inc.

PRINTED IN THE UNITED STATES OF AMERICA

10   9   8   7   6   5   4   3   2   1

PROLOGUE

Talbot Roper tried the door and found it unlocked. This was enough to arouse his suspicion, for front doors were not routinely left unlocked in Denver in this day and age. There was a time when you could leave your doors unlocked, but it had passed. In modern Denver, Colorado, doors had to be kept locked in order to keep not only your belongings safe, but yourself as well. This particular building was in Denver's business district, and at this time of night the door should have been locked. He drew his short-barreled .32 from his shoulder rig and entered.

The message to meet there had come from a woman named Gloria Monahan. Roper did not know her, but she told him she had information he needed for a case he was working on. Unfortunately, he was working on three at the time, so he didn't know which case she was referring to. He decided to go to the meeting and find out.

He entered the building and closed the door behind him. He locked it, so there'd be no surprises after him. Once inside, he paused to give his eyes time to adjust to the dark.

"Hello?" he called.

Roper was aware that he had enemies, and that any of them could have set this up as a trap. Most of his enemies, however, were in prison, sent there by him. If this woman had information germane to one of his cases, he wanted to collect it.

Once his eyes were used to the darkness, he started to move forward. When the floor went out from beneath him and he fell straight down, arms flailing, he knew he'd been duped and felt like a . . .

ONE

As was usually the case when Clint Adams was in Denver, Colorado, he had the cab driver take him from the train station to the Denver House Hotel.

The trip to Denver had been a last-minute thing when the call for help had come, and he hadn't had the time—or the luxury—to simply ride there from Labyrinth, Texas. So he'd been forced to leave behind his Darley Arabian, Eclipse, and take a stagecoach and train. Even so, it had still been three days since he'd picked up the message and almost a week since it had first been sent.

As he entered the hotel, he felt the excitement he always did when he was there. The marble floors, high ceiling, and expensive furnishings matched anything he'd ever seen in San Francisco or New York. And at any given moment—except at night—there were usually fifteen or twenty people in the lobby. They were either guests, or diners in the hotel's fine restaurant, or men who simply enjoyed the ambiance of the Denver House Bar. Whoever they were, there was always activity in the lobby, and Clint liked it. Of course, there were times when he preferred peace and quiet and tranquility, but during those times he stayed away from places like Denver and San Francisco.

However, he was not in Denver by choice this time, so it really didn't matter how he felt.

When he presented himself at the desk, he did not know the clerk, but the man knew him. It was one of the things he enjoyed about the place, that they knew who he was and treated him well.

"Ah, Mr. Adams," the clerk said. "Back with us again. Your usual suite?"

"That'd be fine."

"We've had a managerial change since your last trip, sir," the man said. "The new manager's name is Mr. Sykes. The assistant manager is Miss Hannibal."

"Really?" Clint asked. "Miss?"

"Yes, sir," the man said. "It's the first time we've had a woman in such an exalted position."

The clerk didn't seem too happy about being beneath a woman on the totem pole of importance. He appeared to be in his late thirties, well dressed, with a carefully manicured mustache, the kind that was so thin it made Clint wonder why someone would even have such a thing as a mustache.

"And your name?" Clint asked.

"I am Justin, sir," the man said, handing Clint his key. "Will you be needing assistance with you bag?"

"No," Clint said, picking the carpetbag up from the floor, "I can handle it."

"Very well, sir," Justin said. "Please, enjoy your stay."

"I always do, Justin."

He went up to his two-room suite and dropped his bag on the bed. He walked to the window and looked down at the street. It was too late for him to go to see Talbot Roper. Visiting hours were over and they would not let him into the prison. He took the telegram out of his pocket and read it yet again: REALLY DID IT THIS TIME. NEED HELP. SOON. It was signed: ROPER.

After receiving the telegram, Clint had decided to do

some research. If Roper had really gotten himself in trouble "this time," Clint guessed it would be something newsworthy. His friend Rick Hartman had newspapers from major Texas cities brought in to Labyrinth for him. In both the Dallas newspaper and the San Antonio newspaper, Clint was able to read about his long-time friend, "Prominent Private Detective Talbot Roper," being arrested for murder. . . .

"Wow," Rick said, looking the paper over, "looks like he really did finally do it. You goin'?"

"Hell, yes, I'm going," Clint said. "Roper's one of a handful of men I'd drop everything for."

Hartman stared at him.

"Yes, Rick," Clint said, "you're on that list."

It was not a very big list. Along with Roper and Rick, it included Bat Masterson, Wyatt Earp, and Luke Short. Clint had a lot of friends across the country, but these were the men he considered to be his closest.

Clint had arrived in Labyrinth late the day before and found the telegram waiting at his hotel. It had been sent almost four days earlier.

"When are you leaving?" Rick Hartman asked him.

"Now . . ."

Clint tucked the telegram away in his pocket again, turned, and saw that something had been added to the rooms of the Denver House Hotel since he was last there. There was a telephone on a small table by the bed. He went over to it, picked up the receiver, cranked it up, and waited.

"Front desk."

The voice was tinny, but he thought he recognized it as the voice of Justin, the clerk. Clint had spoken on a telephone before—in San Francisco and New York—but only a handful of times. Each time, he was amazed by it. And he understood they were now present in some Western towns, specifically having heard that the instrument had found its way to Tombstone.

"Justin?"

"Yes, sir."

"This is Clint Adams."

"Yes, sir, how can I help you?"

"I forgot to ask if I had any messages." He had sent a telegram ahead, to tell Roper he would be coming.

"Oh, no, sir, that's entirely my fault. I didn't check . . . yes, you do have one envelope here. I'll have a bellboy run it right up, sir."

"Thank you."

"Would you like anything else?"

"Anything?"

"Anything at all."

"Well . . . could I get a pot of coffee?"

"Of course, sir. I'll send it up with the envelope."

"Thank you, Justin."

"You're very welcome, Mr. Adams."

Clint went into the washroom and found that running water had also been added. He removed his shirt, washed his hands and face, neck and chest, and by the time he was finished, heard a knock at the door.

He walked to it, still bare-chested, opened it, and was surprised to see a woman standing there with a pot of coffee on a tray.

She was equally surprised to see a half-naked man standing in the doorway.

TWO

"You ordered coffee, sir?"

The woman was in her late twenties, wearing a severely cut suit that did little to hide her opulent curves. She had long auburn hair and green eyes that were still wide with surprise.

"Uh, oh, yes, I did," he said, backing away from the door. "Please, come in. Put it anywhere."

She walked in, carrying the tray carefully, as if she were unused to doing so.

"I'm sorry," he said, "let me just get my shirt on."

He went back into the bedroom, got a clean shirt, and pulled it on. He was buttoning it when he came back into the other room.

"Your message is also on the tray, sir," the woman said.

"Thank you," he said. "I, uh, let me give you something—"

"That's not necessary, sir," she said. "I'm not the usual bellboy."

"I can see that."

That made her smile. Her mouth was full-lipped, but had not seemed as wide as it did when she smiled. It lit up her face.

"No, I mean . . . I'm Elizabeth Hannibal."

"The assistant manager?"

"That's right."

"The assistant manager is bringing me my coffee?"

She reached down and tapped the envelope on the tray with her fingernail.

"And your messages. I happened to be going by the desk when you were talking to Justin. I decided to come up myself to meet you."

"I'm flattered."

"You're one of our recurring guests," she said. "I wanted to make sure I knew you on sight." She paused and then said, "Of course, I didn't expect to see so much of you."

"To be fair," he said, "I was expecting a bell*boy.*"

"That's true. How do you like the phone in the room?"

"It's very . . . modern."

"Yes, indeed," she said. "We're trying to improve our services."

"I've always liked this hotel's services," he said. "I'm a bit . . . old-fashioned."

"So . . . you don't like the improvements?"

"They're fine . . . oh, were they your idea?"

"Well . . . I did have to bring something to the table with me in order to get the job."

"Modern ideas."

"Yes."

"Modern ideas are good," he said. "I'm sure people will like them."

"Well," she said, "if you'll excuse me, I'll let you have your coffee while it's hot, and I do have some work to do."

"Thank you for bring it up," he said, walking her to the door. "And it was nice to meet you."

"Yes, you too."

She was a lovely woman, he thought as he closed the door after her. He hoped he hadn't offended her too badly. He also wondered what other modern ideas she had.

He poured himself a cup of coffee, sat in the plush chair the assistant manager had thankfully left in the suites, and opened the envelope. It was a message not from Roper, but from his lawyer, a man named Wilson Perry. It gave Perry's address and asked Clint to come by his office in the morning before going to see Talbot Roper in prison.

He refolded the message, placed it on the tray, and poured himself another cup of coffee. He wondered if Perry knew he was going to arrive today, or if by "in the morning" he'd simply meant whatever morning came after Clint arrived.

In any case, Clint was anxious to see Roper, but thought it was probably a good idea to see the lawyer first.

At the moment, however, he discovered that he was starving. He decided to avail himself of the Denver House's fine restaurant. He left his gun belt on the bedpost, but tucked his .32 New Line into his belt, then donned a jacket. It didn't matter how modern Denver was becoming. He wasn't about to go around unarmed.

THREE

Clint woke early the next morning and had a breakfast in the dining room that was almost as good as the dinner he'd had there the night before. He then went outside and asked the doorman to get him a cab, and gave the doorman the address he wanted to go to.

When he arrived, he found himself standing in front of an impressive brick building in Denver's downtown district. There were four stories, and an elevator to negotiate them. The lawyer's office was on the third floor, and he decided to use the stairs.

When he arrived in front of the lawyer's office he found a door with pebbled glass and the words WILSON PERRY, ATTORNEY AT LAW on it. He entered without knocking.

"Can I help you, sir?" a young woman seated at a small but expensive oak desk asked.

"Yes," he said, "I'd like to see Mr. Perry."

"Do you have an appointment?"

"I believe I do," he said, and handed her the note Perry had left at his hotel.

"Oh, Mr. Adams," she said excitedly. "Mr. Perry has been waiting for you. Come with me, please."

She rose, walked to an unmarked door, and opened it without knocking.

"Mr. Perry, Mr. Adams is here."

A booming voice from within the room said, "Send him right in!" even as Clint was crossing the threshold.

Wilson Perry was coming around from behind his desk with his hand out. He was a big man—not fat, but wide, and thick. Clint put his age in the forties somewhere, the same age group as himself and Talbot Roper.

"Mr. Adams," Perry said, "what a pleasure, sir. A pleasure. I've heard so much about you from Roper."

"Mr. Perry," Clint said. "I've heard nothing about you."

"That's because Roper has never gotten himself in this much trouble before," Perry said, "and has not had to hire me to defend him. Please, have a seat."

Perry returned to his position behind his desk, and Clint sat across from him.

"I know you're probably anxious to see Roper this morning," Perry said, "but I wanted to talk with you first."

"Roper's telegram didn't tell me much," Clint said. "What's going on?"

"He's been arrested for murder."

"For murdering who?"

"A woman named Gloria Monahan."

"What were the circumstances?"

"The police found him at the scene of the murder," Perry said. "They say that as he was leaving the scene the floor gave way beneath him. He fell through, and was unconscious when they found him."

"Did he know the woman?"

"No."

"What was he doing there?"

"He said he got a message from her saying she had some information for him on a case he was working on."

"And what case was that?"

"He doesn't know," Perry said. "At the time he was working on three."

"You must have detectives working on this for you," Clint said. "What do they have to say?"

"No detectives."

"What?"

"Roper says the only man he'll trust to clear him is you."

"But I'm not a detective."

"He says you have the best natural instincts of anyone he's ever met," Perry said.

"And he's willing to bet his life on that?"

"Apparently."

"And you went along with that?"

"What am I supposed to do?" Perry asked, shrugging helplessly. "He told me if I hired anybody else he'd fire me."

"That doesn't make sense."

"I agree." Perry opened his top drawer and took out a piece of paper. "I'll need you to sign this before you start working on this."

"What is it?" Clint accepted it.

"It's a contract that says you work for me," Perry said. "It'll cover you when it comes to the question of confidentiality."

"I have to agree to investigate this, though," Clint said.

"Exactly."

"And I'm not an investigator."

"Maybe we both just have to depend on Roper's opinion of that," Perry said. "He wants you, and I need somebody to work on this. We've already lost a week."

Clint looked down at the contract in his hand, then leaned forward, accepted a quill pen from the lawyer, and signed it.

"There." He pushed it across to Perry.

"Okay," Perry said. "From now on, if you run into the police and they want to know anything, you refer them to me."

"Got it."

Perry stood up. "I'll take you to see Roper now. Once you go in with me, you'll be able to get in on your own in the future."

"Let's go then."

On the way out Perry said, "Maria, we're going to the jail to see Talbot Roper."

"Yes, sir," she said. "Your driver is waiting outside."

Perry looked at Clint and said, "She's a mind reader."

"Every man needs one," Clint said, following Perry out the door.

FOUR

Clint and Perry waited in a room for the guard to bring Talbot Roper in. The room had bare green walls, a table, and two chairs. Perry told Clint to take a seat.

"I'm gonna step out when they bring Roper in," he explained. "Give the two of you some privacy."

"Why is that?"

Perry shrugged. "That's the way Roper wants it. Apparently, you fellas have been friends a long time?"

"A long time, yeah. You?"

"No," Perry said. "Not friends. He's worked for me a time or two, and when he got in trouble he hired me. But I wouldn't say we were friends. The man doesn't seem to have very many."

Before Clint could comment on that, the door opened and he heard the sound of chains. Talbot Roper shuffled into the room, with chains around his wrists and ankles. The guard behind him shoved him once, causing him to stagger, but not fall.

"That's enough of that," Perry snapped, "unless you want me to make a complaint."

The guard scowled, but kept his hands off Roper while the detective sat down.

"Let's go, Officer," Perry said. "We're both stepping out."

"Like hell."

"I have the right to private consultations with my client," Perry said, "and Mr. Adams works for me, so he has the same right."

The guard hesitated, then relented grudgingly and stepped out, Perry right behind him.

"Hello, Clint."

"Tal."

Clint reached out and shook his friend's hand. The usually impeccably turned-out detective looked disheveled, clad in prison grays, his hair a rat's nest and his beard a week or so old. His eyes were red-rimmed and moist. He looked ten years older than he was.

"You look like crap," Clint said.

"Thanks," Roper said. "I feel like crap. Thanks for coming."

"I came as soon as I got your telegram," Clint said. "Unfortunately, I didn't get it right away."

"Doesn't matter," Roper said. "You're here."

"The question is," Clint said, "why am I here?"

"Because you're the only one I can count on, Clint," Roper said. "You're the only person I know who would want me to be innocent, and who'll work hard to prove it."

"I'm not a detective, Tal."

"You have all the instincts," Roper said, "and you have one more thing,"

"What's that?"

"You have me. Now, listen. . . ."

Roper talked for almost ten minutes nonstop, and Clint listened intently.

"Okay," Roper said, "do you have any questions?"

"Yes," Clint said. "Why did you go there alone that night?"

"Who would have gone with me?" Roper asked. "I've

always worked alone, Clint—except for whoever is my secretary at the time."

"And who would that be now?"

"A gal named Hutch."

"Hutch?"

"Jane Hutchinson," Roper said, "but I call her Hutch. Go and see her. She'll give you the files and answer any other questions you might have."

"Tal, what about Perry?"

"What about him?"

"Can I trust him?"

"As long as I'm paying him," Roper said, "you can trust him."

"He said you two weren't friends."

"Not friends, not enemies," Roper said. "Business acquaintances. That's all we have to be."

"Tal . . . I still think you need someone more professional—"

"I want you, Clint," Roper said. "You. I could have gotten a Pinkerton, or somebody like Heck Thomas, but I don't know them. I know you, and I trust you." Roper reached out with both manacled hands and clamped them down on Clint's arm. "I need you to do this for me, Clint. I need you."

"Don't worry, Tal," Clint said. He'd never seen his friend look so desperate before. "I'm going to do it."

Roper sat back, looking relieved. "Knock on the door. They'll let you out and then take me back to my cell."

"Do you need anything, Tal?"

"I've got what I need, Clint," Roper said. "Thanks."

Clint stood up, walked to the door, and knocked.

Once they were outside the prison, Perry asked, "What did he tell you? Anything I should know?"

"Not really," Clint said. "Just some suggestions about how I should start."

"Can I give you a ride back then?"

"I'm going to go to Roper's office to talk to his secretary," Clint said. "I'll just catch a cab."

"All right," Perry said, looking at his watch. "I'm due in court in twenty minutes on another matter. Please keep me informed as to your findings."

"I will."

"It's up to you and me to get him out of this, Clint," Perry said. "To do it, we're going to have to work together."

"I understand that, Mr. Perry."

"Wilson," the lawyer said. "Just call me Wilson. I tell you what, where are you staying?"

"The Denver House."

"Good," Perry said, "they serve the best steak in town. I'll meet you there at eight tonight to compare notes. Dinner will be on me."

"That's fine," Clint said. "See you then."

He watched Perry walk to the street and get into his private carriage, then walked that way himself and waved down a cab.

FIVE

When Clint reached Roper's office he entered without knocking, surprising the woman sitting behind the desk. This wasn't a girl, like those Roper usually had working for him, but a woman in her early thirties. Her eyes widened when he walked in; then she put her hands to her dark hair and said, "Can I help you?"

"Are you Hutch?"

"Jane Hutchinson," she said. "And you are?"

"Clint Adams."

Now her eyes widened again, followed by a smile of relief.

"Oh," she said, putting her hands over her chest, "oh, God, I'm so glad you're here, Mr. Adams. Mr. Roper told me that if anything ever happened to him I was to work with you, listen to you, assist you—"

"When did he tell you this?" Clint asked.

"Last year, when I started working for him," she said. "He told me you were the only man he could really trust, and told me I should do the same."

Clint waked toward her and held out his hand.

"You can call me Clint, Hutch," he said. "It's nice to meet you."

"It's very nice to meet you," she said, shaking his hand. "You'll be wanting to see the files on the three cases Mr. Roper was working on when he was . . . was arrested."

Most of the girls who worked for Roper ended up falling in love with him. Clint wondered if it was the same for this woman.

"I'll need a place to work," he said.

"Yes," she said. "Mr. Roper's office. I've kept it clean. Right in here."

She opened the door and led Clint into Roper's office. As she had said, the place was spotless.

"I can get you whatever you need," she said.

"Well, as you said," he told her, "I'll need the files on the last three cases."

"They're right here."

She opened a file cabinet, took out three folders, and carried them to the desk, where Clint had seated himself. She placed them in front of him.

"What else will you need?" she asked.

"I need some strong black coffee."

"I'll make it myself."

"Thank you, Hutch. After that, I'll just need some time to quietly read these files."

"Yes, sir," she said. "I won't let anyone disturb you."

"Thank you, Hutch."

She nodded and backed out of the room. Several minutes later, he was aware of the smell of coffee. He was halfway through the first file when she entered with a cup of coffee.

"Thanks."

"Can I help?" she asked. "Do you have any questions about the files?"

"No," he said, "not right now, but if I do I'll let you know."

She nodded, turned, and headed for the door.

"Hutch."

"Yes?" She turned, looking at him over her shoulder.

"Can I ask you a personal question?"

She turned completely around, folded her arms beneath her breasts, and said, "Go head."

"Roper usually hired . . . girls for this job," he said. "How come he hired a woman this time?"

She hesitated, then said, "I think I'll take that as a compliment. I told Mr. Roper I wanted to be a detective. He agreed to hire me and train me."

"So you're more than his secretary."

"I'm a secretary . . . and sort of an assistant."

"Okay," he said. "I'll keep that in mind. I'll start getting my own coffee."

"No, no," she said, "that was part of the job. He made that clear when he hired me. We agreed I'd get coffee, go out and get him something to eat, and he'd teach me the business."

"All right," he said. "Understood."

She turned to leave, then turned back.

"Yes?"

"I just wanted to make one other thing clear," she said.

"What's that?"

"Mr. Roper and I were not . . . involved."

He stared at her for a moment, waiting for more, then said, "Okay."

"Okay," she said with a smile, and left.

It took Clint a couple of hours to go through all three files. By the time he was done, his eyes were burning. He sat back in the chair and rubbed them. He was going to have to do what Talbot Roper had told him to when they talked in the jail. . . .

"Talk to everyone involved with all three cases, Clint," Roper had said. "The answer has to be there."

"You don't think this is somebody with an old grudge?" Clint had asked.

"No," Roper had said, "I think this has something to do with one of the three cases I'm working on now. Most of the people who'd hold a grudge against me are inside."

"Most?"

"Yeah," Roper had said. "The others are dead. . . ."

Clint found a piece of paper on the desk, looked for something to write with, then decided to ask Hutch to do something for him. He got up and walked to the connecting door.

"Hutch?"

She looked up from her desk. "Yes?"

"Can you do something for me?"

"Sure."

"I'll need to have the names and addresses of each person involved with all three of Roper's cases," he said.

"Different piece of paper for each case?"

"That would be good."

She opened her top drawer, took out three pieces of paper, and held them out to him.

"Already done," she said.

"That was quick."

"I figured you'd need these in order to talk to everyone connected with the cases."

"Apparently," Clint said, "Roper is training you well."

"He says I'm a natural."

"He's usually a pretty good judge of character," Clint said. "Thanks."

"Sure."

"I'll be in touch."

He headed for the door.

"What hotel are you in?" she asked.

He stopped with the door half open and looked at her.

"Just in case I need to get in touch with you," she added.

"I'm at the Denver House."

"That's a nice place."

"Yeah," he said, "it is."

"Be careful out there," she said. "I mean, if the killer really is someone connected with those three cases . . ."

"I understand," he said. "I'll watch it. Thanks, Hutch."

The man in the doorway across the street watched as a man opened the door to Roper's office halfway, paused, and then stepped out. He didn't know who the man was, but he moved like someone who was sure of himself.

He had not been there when the man went in. Ostensibly, he was there to watch Roper's secretary, but he took it upon himself to follow this new player who had apparently been dealt into the game.

SIX

Clint decided to start questioning people right away, beginning with Roper's three clients. Fortunately, one of them
had an office about three blocks away.

Clayton Royce was a barrel-chested banker who had
hired Roper to find out who was skimming some money
from the deposits. The First Fidelity manager agreed to see
Clint when he presented himself at his office.

"Mr. Adams?" the man said as Clint entered his office.
"Clay Royce. I know of your reputation, sir, but I didn't
know you were a detective."

"I'm not."

"Please," Royce said, after they had shaken hands,
"have a seat. Can I offer you anything? Coffee? Tea? A
drink?"

"No, I'm fine, Mr. Royce," Clint said. "What made you
think I was a detective?"

"My secretary said you were here about Talbot Roper,"
Royce said. "I just assumed you were taking over for him."

"That's not exactly the case, Mr. Royce," Clint said.
"I'm working to clear Roper of a murder charge."

"Yes, I read about it in the papers," Royce said.

"Have you hired another detective yet?"

25

"I don't intend to," Royce said.

"And why is that?"

"I was assured that Talbot Roper was the best detective in the business," the bank manager said. "That's why I hired him instead of going to the Pinkertons."

"But he's in jail now."

"I'll wait until he gets out so he can finish the job."

"You're pretty confident that he's innocent."

"I heard he hired Wilson Perry as his attorney."

"That's true."

"Well, I know Perry is the best in the business."

"Let me get this straight, Mr. Royce," Clint said. "You recognized my name, and Wilson Perry's name, but you had never heard of Talbot Roper until he was recommended to you?"

"That's right."

"Can I ask you who recommended him?"

"Sure," Clayton Royce said. "Wilson Perry."

Outside the bank, the man who had followed Clint from Roper's office found himself a vantage point across the street from where he could watch the front door of the bank. He didn't know if the man he was following was there to make a withdrawal, a deposit, or just talk to someone, but he settled in to wait as long as it took.

Clint and Royce spoke for a little longer, and then the bank manager offered to bring in the suspects.

"Which suspects are those?"

"The ones I suspect of stealing the money."

"I'm not here to look for your thief, Mr. Royce."

"I know that, Mr. Adams," Royce said. "You're looking for whoever framed Mr. Roper . . . but if you happen to find my thief at the same time, there would be a bonus in it for you—and for Mr. Roper, since you're his representative."

"I do want to talk to those people," Clint said, "but I'll do it another time, and in another place."

"Do you have their addresses?"

"I have everything I need, Mr. Royce."

"Well, good," Royce said. "I must say, I quite enjoy having the best detective in the business, and the fastest gun in the West, on my payroll."

"First of all," Clint said tightly, "I'm not the fastest gun in the West, and second, I'm not on your payroll."

Royce held up both of his hands.

"I didn't mean to offend you, sir," he said. "I apologize. I was simply referring to your reputation."

"You can't believe everything you hear, Mr. Royce," Clint said.

"I understand," the banker said. "I stand corrected."

Clint stood up. "Thank you for your time."

Royce stood up and shook hands with Clint again. "Let me walk you out."

Royce's office was on the first floor of the two-story building, and to get to the front door they had to walk the length of the lobby, easily the largest Clint had ever seen in a bank. In fact, it was bigger than some hotel lobbies he'd been in.

"This is a very impressive-looking operation, Mr. Royce."

"Thank you, we're quite proud of it. That's why it burns my ass—sorry—that somebody's stealing money from me."

"From you?"

"Well, from the bank."

At the door, Clint said, "Thank you again for your time."

"Mr. Adams."

"Yes?"

"My curiosity forces me to ask—and I hope you won't

be offended—but if you're not the fastest gun in the West, who is?"

"I don't think I'll say, Mr. Royce."

"Well, then, how many men are there who are faster?"

"Just one, Mr. Royce," Clint said, "just one."

SEVEN

Clint came out of the bank wondering what was going on in the bank manager's head. Somebody was stealing money from his bank, yet he was willing to wait for Talbot Roper to be cleared and released to find out who it was. Something else was going on here.

In addition to that, Clint was already being followed. The man was in a doorway across the street and obviously thought he was invisible. Clint knew that no one had followed him from the hotel to the lawyer's office, from the lawyer's office to the prison, or from the prison to Roper's office. That meant that he'd been picked up at Roper's office, but why had someone been there waiting for him? Unless the man was already there . . . watching Jane Hutchinson?

He decided to go back to Roper's office to check in with Hutch and see if she had seen anyone hanging around the office, but instead of walking, he figured he'd make it hard for the man to follow him. He sauntered along for a block or so, and then quickly waved a cab down and jumped into the back.

"Go!"

"Where to?"

"Just go!" Clint said.

"Okay."

The driver whipped his horse into a frenzy and after they'd gone a block, Clint told him where to go.

"But that's right around the corner," the man said.

"Just go," Clint said.

"Yes, sir."

Clint knew that if the man tailing him was even halfway decent at his job, he wouldn't lose him, but maybe he'd put a scare into the man.

When Clint walked into Roper's office, Hutch looked at him in surprise.

"Back so soon?"

"I have a question for you," he said. "Have you noticed anyone hanging around the office? Or following you?"

"Following me?" she asked. "Someone's been following me?" She actually seemed pleased at the prospect.

"It's possible," he said. "Somebody followed me from here, and I think he was already here when I got here."

She got up from her desk and ran to the window to look, but Clint intercepted her.

"Don't look out the window," he said, grabbing her by the arm.

"Oh," she said, "right. I'm sorry. I was just . . . excited."

"If I remember correctly, there's a back door here."

"Yes," she said, "from Mr. Roper's office."

"All right," he said. "When you go home today, go out that way."

"What are you going to do?"

"I'm going to let the man keep following me for a while, before I turn the tables on him."

"If you find out who hired him, won't you find out who framed Mr. Roper?"

"If somebody hired him," Clint said, "that's about all I'll find out for sure. One might not have anything to do with the other. Can you tell me why somebody might be following you?"

"I have no idea why someone would follow me."

"You're not seeing someone's husband, are you?"

"Absolutely not!" she said, looking shocked. Then, playfully, she added, "I'm not saying I never have, but at the moment I am not."

"No," he said, changing his mind, "if the man was following you, he wouldn't have switched off to me."

She looked disappointed and said, "So I'm not being followed."

"Probably not," he said, "but I still want you to leave by the back door."

"All right."

He put his hand on the doorknob.

"Are you leaving again?"

"Yes," he said. "I still want to see Roper's other two clients before I meet Wilson Perry at my hotel for dinner."

"You're having dinner with Mr. Perry?"

"That's right."

"Can I come?"

"No."

"I've never met him," she said. "Maybe I can help—"

"I'm not sure about Wilson Perry yet, Hutch," he said. "I want to talk to him alone. After all, I just met him today."

"You just met me today," she pointed out.

"I know," he said, "and I'm not quite sure about you either yet."

"What?" She looked appalled. "What can you suspect me of?"

"I don't know," he said. "I'll let you know when I figure it out."

He was out the door before she could say another word.

Outside, the man tailing him was fuming. He didn't like playing games, and that's what this man had just done with him, making him run to catch his own cab and then only taking a cab back to Roper's office.

Obviously, this man wanted him to know that he knew he was being followed. Well, maybe he'd plan a little surprise of his own.

EIGHT

The second client Clint went to see also had an office in Denver, but not in the business district. Harvey Steelgrave was what they would have once called a "town boss." Tombstone, Dodge City, Wichita, Ellsworth, they all had town bosses in their day, men who had their hands and fingers in all kinds of illegal pies. Clint didn't know what they'd call him in Denver, and he also didn't know why Roper would agree to work for the man.

Steelgrave's office was down on the docks, in the back of a small saloon called the River's Edge. Clint entered and immediately drew the attention of the patrons because he didn't fit in.

He went up to the bar and told the bartender, "I'm looking for Harvey Steelgrave."

"Oh, yeah?" the swarthy man asked. "What makes you think he wants to see you?"

"Tell him Talbot Roper sent me."

The bartender recognized that name.

"Wait here."

He came around from behind the bar and went through a door in the back. A couple of men—dockworkers from

33

the look of them—took that as a signal to get up and approach Clint.

They came up to him, one on each side, and crowded him unnecessarily.

"You fellas want to back off?" Clint said. "There's plenty of room for everybody."

"We was thinkin' there ain't no room for you here, friend," one of them said.

"You're definitely in the wrong place," the other one said.

Clint decided not to play games. He put one hand on each man's shoulder and shoved them away from him, hard. Both men were thrown off balance, expecting him to be intimidated by them. They staggered, heard the laughter of the other men in the busy saloon, then righted themselves and started back toward Clint, who was ready to take out his New Line when someone shouted, "Back off!"

Everybody in the place froze, and Clint assumed this was the voice of Harvey Steelgrave. He turned and saw a dark-haired, tall man standing with the bartender.

"Eddie," Steelgrave said to the bartender, "show those two men out, please."

"Hey," one of them said, "we was just—"

"You were bein' rude to a guest of mine," Steelgrave said. "I don't tolerate that. Eddie."

"Come on, you two," Eddie said, "out."

The bartender displayed an impressive wingspan when he spread his arms to usher the two men out of the place. Meanwhile, Steelgrave approached Clint.

"I'm sorry about that," he said. "Would you like to come and talk in my office?"

"Sure, why not?"

"A drink?"

"No," Clint said, "I'm good."

"This way then."

Steelgrave led the way through the place to the office,

and as the door closed behind them, Clint heard the conversations start up again in the outer room.

"You told Eddie that Roper sent you?"

"That's right."

"You saw him in prison?"

"Yes."

"How's he doin'?"

"Not well," Clint said. "It's not a place he's used to being."

"I understand," Steelgrave said. "Even a hard man can crumble the first time he's behind bars."

"Sounds like you're speaking from experience."

Steelgrave grinned and said, "I am. Have a seat."

Once again, Clint observed a man from the other side of his desk. He found himself wishing for a horse beneath him, and he'd only been in Denver for one day.

"Okay," Steelgrave said, "what's this about?"

"You hired Roper to find out who was stealing from you," Clint said.

"That's right."

The town boss and the banker had a lot in common.

"Did you have any suspects in mind when you hired him?" Clint asked.

"I might have given him some names," Steelgrave admitted. "I have a lot of competitors in my business."

"And what is your business?"

Steelgrave laughed.

"Roper knows that," he said. "Didn't he put that in my file?"

"Your file is the slimmest one he gave me," Clint said.

"He's a smart man, that Roper," Steelgrave said. "There are certain things you just don't write down."

"So I understand," Clint said. "Do you think one of your competitors framed Roper for murder to protect himself?"

"Who said he was framed?"

"He did."

Steelgrave apparently decided not to play games.

"Nah, I know he's innocent," he said. "Roper's not the type to kill a woman."

"Who is, Mr. Steelgrave?"

"The city is full of men who would do it," Steelgrave said.

"Point me at somebody."

"I can't do that."

"Why not?"

"Because I wouldn't last very long in business if I started naming names," Steelgrave said. "I just can't do that."

"Roper said you'd help me."

"I will," Steelgrave said. "I like Roper. We have a lot in common."

"Is that why he agreed to work for you?"

"Why shouldn't he work for me?" Steelgrave asked. "You think he's too good for me?"

"I don't know that much about you, Mr. Steelgrave," Clint said, "but judging by what I do know, I'd have to say . . . yes."

Steelgrave stared at Clint for a few moments, and when Clint refused to avert his eyes, the man smiled.

"You and Roper friends?"

"Yes," Clint said, "good friends."

"He picks his friends well then," Steelgrave said. "I think you'll be the one to clear him. I'll help, if I can, but I'm not naming names. Sorry, Mr. Adams."

Clint hesitated, then said, "There is something you can help me with. . . ."

NINE

Steelgrave called the bartender, Eddie, in and told him what Clint Adams wanted. While doing so he actually introduced the two of them. Eddie's last name was Hogan.

"Clint Adams?" he said.

"That's right," Steelgrave replied.

Eddie looked at Clint.

"The Gunsmith?"

Clint didn't answer.

"I never thought I'd see the Gunsmith walkin' around without a gun," Eddie said.

"I'm not."

Eddie studied Clint for a moment, looking for a gun, and then Steelgrave spoke.

"Eddie," he said, "you've got somethin' to do."

"Yes, sir."

Eddie left the room, closing the door behind him.

"A drink while we wait?" Steelgrave asked. "I've got brandy, sherry . . . I can send out to the bar for a beer."

"I'm okay," Clint said.

"I'll have a glass of brandy then . . . if you don't mind," Steelgrave said.

"Go right ahead."

Steelgrave went to a small bar and poured himself a slight measure of brandy into a glass. Clint didn't bother telling the man he should have been using a snifter. Steelgrave tasted it and made a face.

"I hate this stuff."

"Why do you drink it then?"

"I'm tryin' to acquire a taste for the finer things in life."

Clint noticed that Steelgrave was also trying to "acquire" a better command of the English language. Maybe he was hoping to move up the Denver society ladder.

Eddie came back into the room as Steelgrave was putting the brandy down, unfinished.

"So?"

"I looked out the window," Eddie said. "It's one of Mike Brockton's men. His name is Ted Lanigan."

"Brockton?" Clint asked.

"Why would Mike have a man following you?" Steelgrave asked.

"Or why would he have someone watching Talbot Roper's secretary?" Clint asked.

"Maybe you better ask him," Steelgrave said.

"Is he one of the competitors you were talking about?"

"Brockton wants to move in on Mr. Steelgrave's—" Eddie began, but his boss cut him off.

"That's enough, Eddie!" he said. "Go back behind the bar."

"Sure, Boss."

Eddie left, and Steelgrave sat behind his desk.

"Is Brockton one of the names you wouldn't name?" Clint asked.

"Ask Roper about Brockton," Steelgrave said. "Or his lawyer. They'll tell you everything you need to know about him . . . and about others."

"What others?"

"You have the names you need," Steelgrave said. "Brockton . . . Lanigan . . ."

"Well," Clint said, "thanks for that." He stood up. Steelgrave remained seated behind his desk.

"One thing you should remember," Steelgrave added.

"What's that?"

"You're welcome here anytime," Steelgrave said. "As long as you're working to free Roper."

"Have you hired anyone to take Roper's place while he's in jail?" Clint asked.

"No."

"Why not?"

Steelgrave shrugged. "What other detective in this town would work for me?"

TEN

Clint left Steelgrave's office and decided to try something before he left. He went to the bar.

"What'll ya have?" Eddie asked.

Clint could feel a difference in the room. He was willing to bet that Eddie had told everyone there who he was.

"A beer."

"Comin' up."

Eddie put a frothy beer in front of Clint, who picked it up and took a leisurely sip.

"Mr. Steelgrave said you'd tell me about this Lanigan."

"He's an errand boy," Eddie said without hesitation. "A tail. He's a nobody."

"Not a killer?"

Eddie laughed and said, "No. Mike Brockton's got plenty of killers workin' for him, though."

"So I don't have to worry about this Lanigan shooting me in the back?"

"It's not likely," Eddie said. "He's probably only been told to follow you."

Clint had two more sips of beer, then asked, "How much do I owe you?"

"Your money's no good here, Gunsmith."

"Okay," Clint said. "Thanks."

"Sure. See ya."

Clint turned, walked to the door, and left the River's Edge.

As soon as he was gone, Steelgrave came out of his office and walked to the bar. Everyone grew quiet again as Eddie saw his boss coming toward him.

"What did you tell him, Eddie?"

"Uh, just that Lanigan wasn't a killer."

"Nothing else?"

"No, Boss," Eddie said. "He told me you said it was all right. It wasn't?"

"Eddie," Steelgrave said, "when I want you to tell anybody anything, I'll let you know. Understand?"

"Sure, Boss. Sorry,"

"Don't be sorry," Steelgrave said with a wave. "Just . . . shut up sometimes."

Jane Hutchinson was ready to leave work for the day. There really wasn't much for her to do while Talbot Roper was in jail, so she had been reorganizing the filing system in the office. That was why she'd been glad when Clint Adams had finally arrived. Maybe, she'd thought, he'd actually give her something to do.

Well, so far all he'd wanted was coffee, some files, and some lists. And, oh, yeah, he wanted her to leave by the back door.

She, however, was still enamored of the idea that she might have somebody following her. She tried to peek out the front window to see if the man was still there, but she couldn't see anyone—which, of course, didn't mean he wasn't there.

She decided to go ahead and leave by the front door and see what happened. The rooms she rented were within walking distance from the office, in a section that boasted both business and residential buildings. She'd purposely rented some there so she could walk to and from work. Before leaving, however, she went to her desk and removed her two-shot derringer from her top drawer. She placed it inside her drawstring purse, then went to the door. Outside, she took her time locking the office door, but still couldn't see if someone was watching her.

She started walking home, resisting the urge to turn her head and look behind her.

ELEVEN

Clint realized he didn't have time to see Roper's third client today. The man was a rancher with a spread outside of Denver. He'd have to start his day tomorrow by renting a horse and riding out to see Zachary Green.

He got a cab and told the driver to take his time getting him back to his hotel. This time he didn't want to take a chance on losing his tail. He wasn't ready to brace the man, but he wanted to know where he was.

He still had a few hours before he was to meet Wilson Perry for dinner in the hotel restaurant. He decided to do what he hadn't done the day before, when he first arrived. He was going to have a bath, think about what he'd learned so far that day, then go downstairs and have a beer or two while he waited for Perry to arrive.

He stopped at the desk to arrange for a bath to be drawn in his room, then decided to have one beer before, and another after.

Ted Lanigan was still tailing Clint. He watched him go into the hotel saloon, then walked to the front desk.

"Excuse me," he said, "I think I know that man who just went into the saloon. Can you tell me his name?"

"That's one of our more famous guests," the clerk said without thinking. "That's Clint Adams, the Gunsmith."

Lanigan was speechless for a moment, then found his voice and said, "So that's who it is."

"Is that who you thought it was?" the clerk asked, but Lanigan was already walking away.

Clint came back down to the lobby after his bath and was walking by the desk when the clerk beckoned him over.

"What can I do for you, Justin?" he asked.

"I think I may have made a mistake, sir."

"What kind of mistake?"

"Well . . . the kind that might get me fired?"

Clint turned to look at Justin head-on.

"How's that affect me, Justin?"

"Well, a man came in here a little while ago, just after you asked for your bath, and asked me who you were."

"And?"

"And I told him," Justin said. He leaned forward and lowered his voice. "We're not supposed to talk about our guests."

Clint lowered his voice as well. "What did he look like?"

Justin described the man, and Clint realized it was Ted Lanigan, the man who had been following him.

"That's okay, Justin," Clint said. "I know who the man is."

"You won't tell the manager?" Justin asked. "Or Miss Hannibal?"

"No, Justin," Clint said, "I won't tell anybody. In fact, if anybody else wants me tonight, I'll be having a beer at the bar."

"Okay, Mr. Adams," Justin said, "and thanks."

Clint turned and scanned the lobby as he walked across it to the bar. He didn't spot Lanigan, and wondered if the man had given up tailing him after he found out his name.

He walked to the bar, where the bartender recognized him from his earlier visit.

"Back so soon?"

"Your beer was so good I had to have another one before dinner," Clint said.

"Right," the bartender said. He drew Clint a cold mug and set it in front of him. "You're a guest here, ain't you?"

"That's right."

"We started this thing where you can have a drink and charge it to your room," the bartender said. "When you leave, it'll be on your bill."

"Sounds interesting," Clint said, "but I think I'll pay as I go."

The barman accepted Clint's money and said, "Resisting the wave of the future, huh? I don't blame you. I don't much like trolley cars and elevators and telephones myself."

Clint shook his head.

"I don't know what they're going to come up with next," Clint said.

"I know what you mean," the bartender said. "Goddamn railroad's makin' this country smaller as it is. Now we got telegraph wires, and telephones. I used to like it when a man had to ride a horse for days just to see another face."

"You can still do that in certain parts of the West," Clint commented.

"Ah," the bartender said, "this country's gonna be scary in ten years, you mark my words."

"What's your name?" Clint asked. "Just so I know who's words I'm marking."

The bartender stuck out his hand and said, "I'm Mitch Cannon."

"Clint Adams."

"Pleased to meet you, Mr. Adams—wait a minute." The barman released Clint's hand as if it were hot. "Adams?"

"That's right."

"Jesus," the man said, "I got the Old West standin' right here in front of me."

"Well, thanks very much," Clint said, grabbing his beer.

"No, no," Cannon said. "I mean—I didn't mean no offense."

"It's okay, Mitch," Clint said, "none taken."

"I mean, me, I'm in my late twenties, I'm probably gonna live as much of my life in the next century as this one, but you—"

"Okay," Clint said, "now we're getting near the point where I will take offense."

"I just meant—"

"I know what you meant, Mitch," Clint said. "Let's just drop it for now, okay?"

"You know you're the second, uh, famous person I met since I took this job two years ago."

"Oh, yeah?" Clint asked, just to make conversation. "Who was the other one?"

"Bat Masterson," Mitch said. "Fact is, he was here last month. I go maybe a year and a half not meetin' anybody but travelers and businessmen, and then in two months I meet two legends of the West. Ain't that somethin'?"

"It's somethin', all right, Mitch," Clint said. "I'm going to sit at a table and enjoy my beer. It was nice talking to you."

"Yeah, yeah," Cannon said, "you too."

Clint walked to a table in the back and sat his Old West bones down.

TWELVE

Clint was finishing his beer when Wilson Perry walked in and saw him. He was surprised when the man went to the bar and then walked over carrying two beers.

"Don't look so surprised," Perry said. "I can do some things for myself."

"Thanks," Clint said, accepting the fresh beer.

Perry took a healthy swig from his beer and sat back with a sigh. The top button of his shirt was open, but his vest was still buttoned.

"I just need to finish this before we go in to dinner," the lawyer said.

"Rough day?"

"I've got two other cases that are driving me crazy," Perry said. He took another drink, then wiped the back of his hand across his mouth, perhaps revealing something about his past. The silver spoon in his mouth was probably one that he had earned, not one he had been born with.

"What about your day?" Perry asked.

"What can you tell me about Mike Brockton?"

Perry sat forward. "Where did you hear that name?"

"From Harvey Steelgrave," Clint said. "Well, not actu-

ally from him, but from a man who works for him named
Eddie . . . something."

"Steelgrave . . . Brockton . . . you've been busy."

"Do you know a man named Lanigan?"

"No," Perry said, "that name I don't know."

"What about Clayton Royce?"

"First Fidelity Clayton Royce? Of course. He's the
manager of the biggest bank in town. Of course I know
him. I recommended he hire Roper."

Clint wanted to see if the lawyer would admit that.

"I talked to him too," Clint said.

"What about Zachary Green?"

"The rancher," Clint said. "I'm going to ride out to see
him tomorrow morning. You didn't answer my question."

"What question was that?"

"What do you know about Mike Brockton?"

Perry drank some more beer while he composed his
thoughts.

"Brockton came to Denver about three years ago, immediately started working his way up the crime ladder
here in town. He's young, ambitious, smart, and now—after three years—he's almost at the top."

"And who does he have to topple in order to get to the
top?" Clint asked.

"You talked to him," Perry said. "Harvey Steelgrave."

"So do you think Brockton would kill a woman and
frame Roper for it?"

"In a heartbeat," Perry said, "but it would have to be for
business reasons. Nothing personal."

"Nothing personal," Clint said. "Wilson, Roper told me
that all his enemies were either in jail or dead."

"He's right," Perry said. "I did check that out. All of the
men he's helped put away over the past ten years are dead,
and all the ones he's killed are . . . well, still dead."

"Why go back only ten years?"

"Roper's big rep goes back that far," Perry said. "Before that nobody knew who he was, and before that he was still a Pinkerton."

"So there's nobody in Denver with a personal grudge against Talbot Roper?"

"Only if he's been sleeping with somebody's wife," Perry said, "and the husband knows about it."

"So the motive for framing him is business."

"That's the way it looks."

"And the men we're dealing with—the banker, the outlaw, and the rancher—all have enough money to have had this done."

"Oh, yes."

"Well, can't you use that?" Clint asked. "Create reasonable doubt in court with that?"

"Roper doesn't want to go to court," Perry said. "He wants you to get him out of jail."

"How am I supposed to do that?"

"I don't know," Perry said. "But why don't we continue talking about this over dinner?"

Once they were seated in the restaurant and their orders had been taken, Perry looked at Clint and said, "You asked a question."

"I did," Clint said. "How am I supposed to get him out?"

"Find the real killer," Perry said. "It's as simple as that."

"Aren't the police working on it?"

"Well, no," Perry said. "They think they have their killer, remember? They have Roper."

"Perry," Clint said, "you need a real detective on this."

"Well," Perry said, "you're in charge of this investigation. If you want to hire help, do it."

"You'll pay for it?"

"Oh, no," Perry said. "Roper is footing the bills. He'll pay for it."

"So I can bring somebody in to work with me?"

"If you like," Perry said. "Why not? I don't care what you do, as long as we get him out."

Perry broke off as the waiter set down their dinners.

"Let's put this discussion off until dessert, shall we?" Perry asked. "I like to concentrate on my dinner. It's one of my only vices."

"Eating dinner?"

Perry smiled. "Having the time to enjoy it."

THIRTEEN

After dinner, Clint invited the lawyer back into the bar for another beer.

"No, thank you," Perry said. "I need to get home and get some rest. I've got to start all over again early in the morning."

"I'll walk you out."

"I know the way."

"I know you do," Clint said. "I want to see if you've got anyone following you."

"Might have my own Ted Lanigan, huh?" Perry asked. "I don't know why anyone would be following me, but okay. Let's go."

They walked to the door, and Perry asked the doorman to get his driver.

"See anything?" he asked Clint.

"Not right now."

"Well," Perry said, "if you see something after I pull away, let me know in the morning, all right? I'll be stopping by my office from nine to ten, but then I'll be in court."

"About Roper?"

"No, another case," Perry said. "Two cases, in fact. I have several cases. Here's my driver. Good night."

Perry walked down to the street and left in his carriage before Clint could ask him if any of his other cases involved the banker, the outlaw, or the rancher.

Clint was sitting in the bar drinking one last beer when Elizabeth Hannibal came walking in. She stopped at the bar to talk to the bartender for a moment, then saw Clint and walked over to him. He noticed the bartender watching her walk with a lascivious grin on his face.

"Mr. Adams," she said. "Enjoying your stay?"

"First day was kind of busy," Clint said, "but I'm relaxing now. Why don't you join me?"

"Thank you."

She turned to wave to the bartender, and as she did, the man made his face go blank.

"Coffee, Mitch," she said.

"Comin' up, Boss."

She sat opposite Clint as the bartender hurried over and put her coffee in front of her.

"Just the way you like it, Miss Hannibal."

"Thanks, Mitch."

Before the bartender went back to the bar, he looked at Clint and, while Elizabeth couldn't see his face, licked his lips and waggled his eyebrows.

"What made your day so busy?" she asked.

"Lots of people to talk to," Clint said, watching the bartender walk back to the bar. He suddenly liked Mitch Cannon a lot less.

"You didn't tell me what you were doing in town."

"We didn't really talk that long," he said. "I'm here to help a friend who's in trouble."

"Do you do that a lot?" she asked. "Help friends in need?"

"Probably more than I should."

"Makes you a good friend to have then."

"I like to think so."

She hadn't lifted her cup to her lips yet, but was running her index finger around the rim.

"So when did you become assistant manager?" Clint asked.

"About six months ago. I was a supervisor for a while—front desk personnel, the maids, that sort of thing—but when the new manager took over, he promoted me."

"I haven't met him."

"I'll have to introduce you tomorrow," she said. "You probably won't like him. Nobody does."

"Don't you?" he asked. "He promoted you."

"He did," she said, "but he's still an unlikable type. Fussy little man with lots of rules."

"Sounds like he's perfect for his job."

"Oh, he is," she said. "I respect him for that."

"What about . . . other men?"

"Like?"

"The desk clerk . . . the bartender . . . boyfriend?"

"Justin," she said, "is a back-stabber. He hates women and wants my job. Then there's Mitch over there, who doesn't know that I know all about the faces he makes behind my back."

"I wondered about that."

"He's a good bartender."

"And what about the other? Boyfriend?"

"I'm more interested in men than boys," she said, "but right now, there's nobody."

"Any prospects?"

She smiled. "Not that I know of. How about you? Any women?"

"Lots of them."

"Anyone special?"

He smiled.

"Oh," she said, "lots of them."

He shrugged.

"So, you're that kind of man?"

"What kind is that?"

"No attachments?"

"It's usually easier that way," he said. "Wherever I am, I'm destined to leave."

"But not for a while, right? I mean, your friend needs help and that'll probably take a while, right?"

"Right."

She touched her hair.

"So . . . do you have any plans for the rest of the evening."

"No," he said. "No plans for the rest of the evening . . . or the night."

She smiled.

FOURTEEN

Clint had to admit that when he first came to the Denver House yesterday he never expected to be in bed with the assistant manager the next night—not that he minded.

When they got to his room, she turned into his arms and they shared a long, gentle kiss.

"It's been a while since I met a man I wanted to be with," she whispered.

"I'm flattered."

She bit down on his bottom lip and said, "Don't disappoint me."

"I don't intend to."

He stripped her business suit off to reveal a very unbusinesslike body beneath it. Certainly not the kind of body you'd expect to find on a hotel manager—or assistant manager.

Her breasts were full and heavy, the nipples large and dark brown, distended now as he held her in his hands. She had wide hips and a pleasantly cushioned behind. Her skin was very smooth and pale and, as he rubbed his face over her, fragrant.

When he had her tamed, he pressed her back to the bed and then down onto her back. From that position she watched him undress, and when his erect penis came into sight, she licked her lips. It was every bit as lascivious as it had been when the bartender did it.

He straddled her, pressed his erection to her belly, felt her pubic hair tickling his testicles. As he bent to kiss her, he felt her legs come up and wrap around him.

"Not yet," he said as she tried to draw him to her. "You said it's been a while. Relax and enjoy it."

"I tell you what," she whispered into his ear. "You give it to me now, hard and fast, and next time I'll relax and enjoy it."

He propped himself up, with a hand on either side of her, and asked, "And when will the next time be?"

She smiled, put her arms around him, and said, "I guess that depends on how quickly you recover."

He smiled, reached down, and took his penis in his own hand. He pressed the head against her, moved it up and down, but she was already wet enough for him to slide right into her.

"Ooh, yeah," she said, "now give it to me, come on . . . and do it hard . . . I won't break."

He started fucking her then, hard enough that he knew they were going to prove or disprove that statement. . . .

"Now?" she asked a little while later. "Again? Already?"

"You said it was up to me, remember."

"Yes, but . . . I didn't think you'd recover this quickly."

He kissed her breast, bit her nipple, asked, "Disappointed?"

She grabbed his head, laughed—a wicked sound that sent chills up his spine—and said, "Pleasantly surprised."

He moved to her other breast, kissed it tenderly, licked the nipple, then bit it. Next he ran his tongue down between her breasts and kept going, over her belly, stopping briefly at her belly button, then working his way down to her crotch. He breathed on her pubic hair, which made her squirm and dig her butt into the mattress.

She reached down to cup the back of his head as his tongue flicked out to taste her. She moaned and pressed his face harder to her. Her pubic hair rubbed against his face as he drove his tongue into her, and her butt came up off the bed. Her scent was heady, intoxicating, a combination of the natural scent of her skin, some kind of perfume, and her wetness. . . .

She moved her hips in tandem with his tongue, but then he slid his hands beneath her butt to cup her cheeks and hold her still. His tongue found her rigid clit and began to flick it, and she went wild beneath him. She released his head and set her palms down on the bed, then closed her hands into fists and gathered the sheet up.

Suddenly, she began to grunt. He felt her legs begin to tremble, and then her belly. Then she started to growl, almost like an animal. He felt something squirt against his tongue, something tart, and then she started to scream. She quickly turned her face into the pillow to muffle the sound, but it went on for a while as she bucked beneath him and he tried to stay with her.

She was still thrashing when he released her. He got to his knees, took her legs in his hands and spread them, and drove himself into her again. He'd meant to go slower, but her reactions had inflamed his own lust. His penis was harder than he recalled it ever being, felt like it was about to burst. He began to move in and out of her slowly, holding her by the hips. Her face was still turned into the pillow, and she was moaning now as the waves from one orgasm subsided and another began.

He took her in long, hard strokes and she reached out for him, raked his back with her nails, slid her hands down to cup his buttocks and pull him into her, harder and harder. He began to grunt with the effort; his throat started to get dry from the heavy breathing. Both their bodies were slick with sweat and they were both grunting now. Clint felt his excitement mounting higher and higher, and yet as he drove into her over and over again, his prick simply felt like it was getting harder and harder. He felt like he could fuck this woman all night, except he found himself wondering if his heart would stand up to that.

Maybe they were going to find out.

FIFTEEN

"Who told you to leave?"

"It's night," Lanigan said. "He's asleep."

"You better hope he is," Mike Brockton said. "When you found out who he was, you should have got a message to me."

"I tailed him all day," Lanigan said, "and only found out tonight he was Adams."

"You saw him go to the bank, and then down to Steelgrave's place," Brockton said.

"That's right."

They were in Brockton's office in an old part of Denver he liked. He'd chosen to stay off the docks, and out of the business district, when he set up his office. From there, he hoped to take control of both of them.

"He went to First Fidelity?"

"Yeah."

"Did you see who he talked to?"

"No."

"Shit."

Brockton wondered if it had been the bank manager, Clayton Royce, or another bank employee.

"Who else did you see?"

"Roper's lawyer."

"Perry?"

Lanigan nodded. "I looked in the lobby, saw them going into dinner together. I got a closer look, and they were sitting together."

"Then what?"

"Then Perry left."

"Did Adams go to the door with him?"

"Yeah."

"He see you?"

"Not that time."

"But he saw you sometime during the day."

"I'm pretty sure."

Brockton sat back in his chair, scratched an itch on the top of his head.

"I'll bet somebody at the River's Edge told him who you were," he said.

"If they did, why wouldn't he brace me then?" Lanigan asked, puzzled.

"That's a good question."

"You want to put somebody else on him tomorrow?"

"No," Brockton said, "I'll put somebody else on the girl. You stay on Adams."

"If he sees me—"

"I want him to see you, Ted," Brockton said. "I want him to know he's still being followed. I want to see what he's gonna do."

Lanigan licked his lips nervously. "He might kill me."

"He's not gonna kill you," Brockton said, "not without a good reason."

"Boss—"

Brockton pointed his finger at his man.

"Just stay on him and don't give him any reason to kill you," he said. "Got it?"

Lanigan hesitated, then said, "Yeah, I got it."

"Get some sleep, and pick him up in the morning."

Lanigan stood up to leave.

"Be at his hotel at 7 A.M., just in case he gets a real early start for himself."

"That don't give me much time to sleep."

"Then stop standin' there complainin' about it and go get it done."

"Yes, sir."

As Lanigan left, Brockton, who knew Clint Adams by reputation only, wondered if it would be the last time he saw the man. Didn't really matter. A Ted Lanigan would not be hard to replace at all.

SIXTEEN

Clint awoke the next morning with a hotel assistant manager down between his legs.

By the time he woke, she had his dick hard already and was sucking on it. She slid one hand beneath his testicles to cup them gently, and slid the other hand up over his chest.

She giggled with him still in her mouth, then released him but didn't go very far. She pinned his erection to his belly with her chin.

"I was wondering when you would wake up," she asked.

"You tired me out last night, Elizabeth," he told her. "I slept like the dead, which is unusual for me."

"Hmm," she said. She lifted her chin, then licked the length of him, from bottom to top. When she got to the top, that sensitive place just beneath the head, his penis jumped.

"Want to go back to sleep?" she asked.

"Hell, no," he said.

"I didn't think so," she said, and engulfed him in her hot mouth again.

"Breakfast?" he asked as he watched her get dressed.

"I have to get dressed and go to work."

"You are getting dressed," he said, "and doing it very nicely too."

"No, I have to put something else on," she said. "I can't be seen walking around in the same clothes I had on yesterday. People would start to talk."

"So you have to go home?"

"No," she said, sitting on the bed so she could put on her shoes. "I have some clothes here. I just have to change." She finished dressing and looked at him. "But you can have breakfast. Tell them to charge it to your room."

"I like to pay as I go."

"If you have it put on your room, I'll have it taken off," she said.

"Is that what I'm worth?" he asked. "A breakfast?"

"How about if I cover all your meals while you're here?" she asked, leaning close to him. She still smelled of perfume and sex.

"Won't that get your boss mad?"

"I'm in charge of the guests," she said.

"Then I accept your most indecent offer."

"Good." She kissed him on the mouth, then got up and walked to the door. "This is going to be the best stay you ever had at the Denver House, Mr. Adams."

He leaned back and put his hands behind his neck.

"I was just thinking the same thing."

He took her up on her offer of breakfast. He dressed and went down to the restaurant. There was a different man at the desk, but he nodded to Clint as if he knew who he was. Or maybe he just nodded that way to every guest.

While Clint was eating his steak and eggs, a man entered the restaurant and looked around. He was a small, nattily dressed man with a bow tie and vest under his suit. He looked to be all of five feet six, and probably weighed in at about 140 pounds. When he spotted Clint and started toward him, Clint ventured a guess that this was Mr. Sykes, the new manager.

"Mr. Adams?"

"That's right."

"Please," the man said, "don't interrupt your breakfast. I simply wanted to introduce myself. Bruce Sykes, manager of the Denver House Hotel."

"Nice to meet you, Mr. Sykes," Clint said. He paused in his eating to shake hands with Sykes.

"I hope your stay in our hotel has been satisfactory up until now," the smaller man said.

"It has," Clint said. "Your assistant, Miss Hannibal, has made me feel very comfortable."

"Excellent," Sykes said, "excellent. If there's anything you need that she can't provide, please let me know."

Clint hesitated, then said, "I don't think that'll happen, but I'll keep your offer in mind."

"Very good," Sykes said. "Please, enjoy your breakfast."

Sykes almost clicked his heels, then turned and left, acknowledging several of the other guests along the way.

Ted Lanigan had been standing outside since 7 A.M., just as Mike Brockton had ordered. Now he decided to come inside, take a look, and see if Adams was having breakfast. He spotted Clint sitting at a table, talking to a short man in a bow tie. Satisfied that he hadn't missed him, he went back outside to wait for him to leave the hotel.

After breakfast, the waiter came over and Clint said, "I'd like to charge this to my room, please."

"No problem, sir," the man said. "I'll take care of it."

"Thank you."

Clint left a tip on the table for the waiter and went out to the lobby. He paused a moment to look it over, and didn't see the man who had been tailing him the day before. He looked at the front door, then walked to the desk.

"Yes, sir?" the new clerk asked. "Can I help you?"

"I need to rent a horse."

"Of course," the man said happily. "I can help you with that. We have a stable right behind us."

"That's good."

"What color would you like?"

"What?"

"What color horse?"

"I don't want to order a horse by color," Clint said.

"Oh." The man looked confused.

"I want to see what you've got and choose my own."

"All right," the man said, "very well, I suppose we can do . . . uh, I'll have a bellboy take you back there."

"Thank you."

"Oh, and how would you be paying for this?"

Clint hesitated only for a moment and then said, "I'd like to put it on my bill."

SEVENTEEN

Clint followed a bellboy to the stables, where he was given his choice from eight horses. The hotel's liveryman said they usually had twelve but that two buggies and one buckboard had been taken out just that morning.

"You don't rent out your saddle mounts to pull buggies, do you?" he asked.

"It don't matter," the man said. "Somebody wants a buggy, we hook up a horse. They want a saddle mount, we toss a saddle on one of 'em. They're all good horses."

"They're not going to stay that way if you keep doing what you're doing," Clint said.

He took a look at the remaining eight horses and picked out the best of the lot, which he considered to be poor.

"Need a saddle?" the man asked.

"Yes," Clint said, afraid of what he would end up with there, "I'm afraid I do."

"Lemme show ya what we got. . . ."

The choice of saddles was even worse than the choice of horses, but he made do.

There were two items on his list of things to do before he headed out to Zachary Green's ranch. The first was easy

to achieve. He rode the horse around to the front of the hotel so that Ted Lanigan could see him riding away. That
was all he wanted to do, frustrate the man. Then he headed
for Talbot Roper's office.

Lanigan was caught flat-footed when Clint came riding by
on a horse. He couldn't run after him—he'd never keep up.
He couldn't get a horse of his own—there was no time. All
he could do was try to wave down a passing cab, but in that
area the drivers gave first choice to the hotel doorman, so
several of them simply drove right by Lanigan as he waved
frantically. In the end, he knew he was done. All that was
left was for him to figure out what to do next.

By the time Jane Hutchinson returned to work that morning, she was thoroughly depressed about not having been
followed—not the night before, on the way home, and not
that morning on the way to the office. She was sulking behind her desk when she heard the door open and saw Clint
Adams walk in.

Clint reined his rented in and dismounted in front of
Roper's office. He tied the horse off to a metal hitching
post and went inside. Jane Hutchinson was seated at her
desk, and he had the feeling she wasn't very happy right up
to the moment she smiled at him.

"Clint! Good morning."

"Morning, Hutch."

"How did everything go yesterday?" she asked. "And
last night?"

"Everything went fine. I assume you got home all right
last night?" he asked.

"Yes, fine," she said. "Nobody followed me at all."

"Well, that's good, isn't it?"

"I suppose."

"Believe me," he said. "It's good."

She looked glum, but then brightened and asked, "What's on the agenda today?"

"I'm going to ride out and talk to Zachary Green," he said, "but I didn't see any directions to his place in his file."

"Oh," she said, "it didn't occur to me that you would be riding out there. I can get you the directions from the master file."

"Master file?"

"Why, yes," she said. "The files I gave you were ones I made especially for you. I put in them the things I thought you would need."

"So there's information that's not in the files I have?"

"Well, yes, but—"

"Hutch," Clint said, "I need as much information as I can get. That means I need everything that's in those files."

"I'm sorry," she said, "I was trying to simplify your—"

"Are there directions to Green's ranch in the main file?"

"Yes," she said. "I can copy them for you, if you'll give me a few min—"

"Just let me have the master files. All of them."

"B-but, Mr. Roper doesn't like for the files to leave—"

"Hutch," Clint said, "if I don't clear Roper there won't be any need for any files, because he won't be coming back."

"Oh . . . of course . . ."

She went to the file cabinet, took out three files, and handed them to Clint. They were each just a little thicker than the files he already had.

"Do you have a pouch, a leather pouch, or a saddlebag—"

"Mr. Roper uses this."

She got him a leather pouch that looked like half a saddlebag.

"That's good enough. Thanks."

He turned to leave.

"But . . . where are you going?"

"Out to the Green ranch."

"When will you be back?"

"Hopefully," he said, "before dark tonight, depending on how far it is and how much talking we do."

"Can't I—" She stopped.

"What?"

"Can't I come with you?"

"No," Clint said. "I rented a horse from my hotel and I have it right outside. I've got to go now. I'm sorry, but you'll have to stay here."

"But what if, um, a man comes back, or—"

"I tell you what you can do."

"What?"

Clint found her eagerness annoying. It belonged on a much younger woman.

"Do you know where Wilson Perry's office is?" he asked.

"Of course."

"Go there, and tell him where I've gone. Tell him I'll talk to him later, when I get back."

"That's it?"

"That's it, Jane," he said. "That's the job I have for you. Take it or leave it."

EIGHTEEN

It was over an hour's ride to the ZG spread of Zachary Green. According to the file Clint had read—which he now knew was not the main file—Green had hired Talbot Roper to find out who was rustling his cattle. Clint wondered why Green would choose to hire Roper rather than a stock detective.

He also wondered, during his ride, if Jane Hutchinson had been trying to keep information from him by preparing special files just for him. He was going to have to read the master files, compare them to his, and then take that subject up with Roper. But for now he needed to concentrate on Zachary Green and his ranch.

And apparently, his men, because at that moment about half a dozen of them were approaching him, and they didn't look friendly.

"Hold it right there!" one of them called.

Clint decided to rein in and not risk triggering a gunfight where one was not necessary.

The six men surrounded him, with the spokesman directly in front of him.

"State your business."

"I'm here to see Zachary Green."

"For what purpose?"

"I'm not sure that concerns you."

The man sat straight up in his saddle and puffed out his chest. Clint knew he was either going to be threatened, or challenged.

"My name is Seth Jenks," the man said. "I'm the foreman of the ZG Ranch. If you want to see Mr. Green, you have to go through me first. Now identify yourself."

"My name is Clint Adams," he said, "and I'm here representing Talbot Roper."

"Roper?" For the moment, Roper's name seemed to mean more to Jenks than his own, which suited Adams.

"That's right."

"He's in jail."

"That's why I'm here and he's not."

"What's your business with Mr. Green?" Jenks asked. "He's already replaced Roper."

"I'm trying to clear Roper of the murder charge he's under," Clint said. "I would just like some of Mr. Green's time to ask him a few questions."

"Are you willing to give up your gun?"

"No."

"Why not?"

"I gave you my name," Clint said. "You know why."

"Let him keep his gun."

Clint turned to look at the man who had spoken. He was a young man, about thirty, unremarkable-looking, but he sat his horse with great confidence.

"Why should we?" Jenks asked.

"Because it would be too damaging to us to try and take it," the other man said. "Besides, I don't think he's here to harm anyone . . . are you, Mr. Adams?"

"No," Clint said. "I explained why I'm here."

"Just to ask some questions," the second man said.

"Right."

The second man looked at Jenks.

"I don't see anything wrong with that, Jenks," he said. "We can accompany him back to the ranch."

Jenks matched gazes with the other man, and the foreman was the one who looked away first.

"All right," Jenks said to Clint. "Ride along with us."

Clint turned to the other man and said, "Thanks."

"No problem."

"Mr. Adams," Jenks said, "this is the man Mr. Green hired to replace Talbot Roper. Meet Tom Horn."

NINETEEN

The riders kept Clint in their circle as they rode up to the ranch house. Clint could see that Zachary Green had money. This house had been built especially for him, and it resembled the mansions Clint had seen in the Deep South.

No one spoke to Clint as they rode in, but Tom Horn rode the closest to him.

Clint had heard of Tom Horn—good things, and bad things. Horn was supposed to be an excellent stock detective, but they said he sometimes took the law into his own hands.

When they had all stopped in front of the house, the foreman dismounted and told the other men to see to the horses. Horn dismounted and handed the reins of his horse to another man.

"I wanna hear this," he said to Jenks, who simply shrugged. Clint had the impression that they both worked for Green, but that Jenks did not hold any rank over Horn, even as foreman.

They mounted the steps to the front porch and then Jenks turned to face them.

"If you'll wait here, I'll tell him you're here."

"Fine," Clint said.

Once Jenks had gone inside, Clint asked Horn, "When did they bring you in?"

"I've been here a couple of days."

"Making any headway?"

"Still feelin' my way around," Horn said. "Too bad about what happened to Roper."

"Do you know him?"

"I know of him," Horn said. "Man's got a big rep as a detective."

"He's the best."

"His rep ain't as big as yours, though."

"Mine's got nothing to do with being a detective."

"I know that," Horn said. "Your reputation is with a gun."

"And yours is too," Clint said.

"Not like yours," Horn sad. "I ain't no Gunsmith—not yet anyway."

"That's nothing to aspire to, believe me," Clint said to the younger man.

"Aspire?"

"It's not something you should want to be," Clint said, clarifying his statement.

"You don't like who you are?" Horn asked.

"I like myself fine," Clint said. "It's how other people see me I don't like."

"I know what you mean," Horn said. "Sometimes we got no control over that."

Clint was about to respond when Jenks reappeared at the front door, holding it open behind him.

"Mr. Green says he'll see you in the sittin' room," Jenks said. "This way."

Both Clint and Horn followed Jenks into the house, across a wide entry hall, and into what was obviously the sitting room.

"Well, well," said the man standing in the center of the room. "This is a momentous occasion. The Gunsmith and

Tom Horn in the same room. Do you fellas knows each other?"

"We just met," Horn said.

"Well, then, let me introduce myself." He said "mah-self," and the thick Southern accent explained the appearance of the house. "Ah am Zachary Green, sir. Ah I'm pleased to meet you." He extended his hand to Clint, who shook it.

"Please, can I get either of you gentlemen a drink?" Green asked. "Some sherry perhaps?"

"Don't do it," Horn said to Clint. "It's vile stuff."

"Well," Green said, "it is an acquired taste."

"None for me, thanks," Clint said. "I won't take up too much of your time, Mr. Green."

"Not at all," Green said. "Jenks tells me you're representing Talbot Roper. I'd like to do anything I can to help him. However, I'm not sure what you mean by 'represent.' Are you . . . an attorney?"

"I work for his attorney."

"I see."

"But Roper and I are old friends," Clint said. "I'm trying to clear him of the charges against him."

"Well, then," Green said, spreading his hands, "I am at your disposal, sir."

He was dressed for the South, not for a Colorado ranch. His pants and shirt were white, as was his jacket, and Clint was sure that the hat would match. He wore a black tie, though, which at the moment was not tied. He appeared to be in his early forties, and Clint wondered if the man had made his fortune, or inherited it.

"Please, have a seat," Green said. "If I can't persuade you to have a drink, the least I can do is make you comfortable."

Clint sat down in an overstuffed armchair that felt as if he was sitting on a cloud.

"Kinda grabs hold of ya, don't it?' Horn asked.

"I see what you mean," Clint said.

"That's why I stand," Horn said. "Can't stand fancy chairs."

"Mr. Horn's tastes are rather pedestrian," Green said, seating himself in a similar chair, across from Clint, "but I understand he is very good at what he does."

"That's what I heard too."

"Anyway," Zachary Green said, "you said you had questions . . . fire when ready, sir."

TWENTY

Clint's main reason for meeting the banker, the outlaw, and
the rancher was to get a sense of who they were, to try to
"feel" whether they were the type of men who would frame
Talbot Roper for murder if it suited their purposes. Just because they were his clients did not mean they weren't out
to get him.

So his questions to Zachary Green were much the same
as those to Roper's other two clients. Who did he suspect
of rustling? Did he know of anyone who would want to
frame Roper? Unlike the other two clients, however, Green
obviously was not willing to wait for the detective to be
cleared in order to come back and work on his problem.

"That's the reason I hired Mr. Horn." Green said. "I
need to resolve this as soon as possible."

"I understand that."

Clint noticed that Horn watched him closely during the
short question-and-answer session.

"Well," Clint said, standing, "I don't think I have any
more questions."

Zachary Green also stood and gave Clint an admiring
look.

"You came out here just to size me up, didn't you?"

"Partially," Clint said. "I also needed to get a horse under me again, and this seemed as good a way as any."

"Can't blame you for that," Green said. "I have to get up on a horse every so often myself. Let me show you to the door."

If he somehow signaled Jenks and Horn to wait for him, Clint didn't see it, but the two men remained in the sitting room while Green showed Clint the way out.

"I understand Mr. Roper has engaged Wilson Perry as his attorney," the rancher said on the way to the door.

"That's right."

"Well, with both you and Perry working for him, I don't think Roper has anythin' to worry about, do you?"

"He's in a bad position, Mr. Green," Clint said. "Personally, I think he's got a lot to worry about."

"Well," Green said, "I'm sure things will turn out fine for him."

He opened the door for Clint and shook hands again.

"If there's anything else you think I can do for you, please don't hesitate to let me know."

"I won't," Clint said. "Thank you for your time."

As the door closed behind him, Clint saw that his horse was waiting for him right at the bottom of the steps.

Tom Horn's mixed reputation concerned him, but as he mounted up and headed back to Denver, he realized that he'd be doing Horn the same disservice people did to him if he judged him solely on his reputation.

Zachary Green returned to the sitting room, where Jenks and Tom Horn were both waiting for him. He left them waiting while he poured himself more sherry. He turned then and gestured at Tom Horn with the bottle.

"No, thanks," Horn said.

He set the bottle down without offering any to Jenks.

"So, what did you think?" Green asked.

"About what?" Horn asked.

"I don't see where his big rep—" Jenks started, but Green cut him off.

"I was talking to Mr. Horn, Jenks. In fact, that's all. You can go on about your work."

Jenks looked at Horn, who simply shrugged, and then the foreman left, with heavy, angry steps.

"I meant, what did you think of Mr. Clint Adams, the Gunsmith?" Green asked. "Were you impressed?"

"We only talked for a short time," Horn said. "I don't think I was any more impressed with him than he was with me."

"Well," Green said, "he's been a legend a lot longer than you have."

"I'm no legend," Horn said.

"You're modest about it," Green said. "That's one reason why I like you, Horn."

"I need to get back to work."

"Of course, of course," Green said. "I was just concerned . . . do you think Adams could be involved in this in any way?"

"Nothin' in his reputation says he's a rustler," Horn said. "Also, if he'd been in the area longer than a couple of days, I'm sure you would've heard about it. Man like that can't just blend into the background."

"Perhaps not," Green said.

"By the way," Horn said, "you should probably treat Jenks with a little more respect. After all, he is your foreman."

Green stopped with his glass partway to his mouth and looked at Horn over the rim.

"Exactly," Green said, "he's my foreman, my employee. I'll thank you not to try and tell me how to treat my people."

"Suit yourself," Horn said. Mentally he added, as long as you never try to treat me like that. "I'll be on my way."

"Yes," Green said, "I'm sure you need to be out there in order to catch these rustlers."

"I'll let you know when I have some information for you," Horn said, and left the room.

Outside, Jenks fumed. He didn't like the way Zachary Green treated him, but he was the man's foreman, and he knew that Green kept a definite line between himself and his men. However, being treated that way in front of Tom Horn made it worse.

Green hadn't wanted to hear Jenks's opinion of Clint Adams, but the foreman didn't see where Adams was anything so special. Then again, he didn't see what was so special abut Tom Horn either.

If Green had left the rustling problem up to Jenks, if he had shown the man any degree of respect, Jenks could have wrapped up the situation before long. But no, first he had to hire Talbot Roper, and then when Roper got himself into trouble, he had to bring in Tom Horn.

Jenks turned as the front door opened and Horn stepped out.

"Goin' back out?" Jenks asked.

"Yep."

"Want me and the men to go with you again?"

"No," Horn said. "This time I think I want to ride around alone for a while."

"Suit yourself."

Horn descended the steps and walked over to the stable to get his horse. Jenks watched him, tracking him with tense eyes until he disappeared from sight.

TWENTY-ONE

Given the time Clint had spent riding out to Green's ranch and the amount of time it would take him to ride back, the trip really hadn't accomplished much beyond meeting the man. He had discovered that Green was not as enamored of Talbot Roper's abilities as his other two clients were, since he'd wasted no time in replacing him with Tom Horn. Beyond that, Clint hadn't learned much.

Clint was riding at a leisurely pace, not wanting to press the rented animal too much, when he heard the sound of a horse's hooves coming up behind him fast. He turned, his hand hovering near his gun, and saw Tom Horn riding up on him.

"Mind if I ride with you a spell?" Horn asked.

"Why would you want to do that?"

Horn shrugged. "Thought we might talk."

"About what?"

"This and that."

"Suit yourself," Clint said. "If you want to ride along I have no objection."

They turned their horses and headed toward Denver.

• • •

Jenks had seen Tom Horn leave the ranch and wondered where the man was going in such a hurry, so he grabbed his own horse and followed him. Now he watched as Horn caught up to Clint Adams. The two exchanged a few words and then started riding toward Denver together. Jenks wondered if the two men had really just met or if they'd known each other before.

He didn't see any reason to follow further, though, so he wheeled his horse around and rode back to the ranch.

Clint and Horn made some small talk, exchanged the names of some mutual acquaintances, and didn't discuss anything of importance for half an hour.

Finally, Clint said, "Why do I have the feeling you're feeling me out for some reason?"

"Maybe 'cause I am."

"So you're here in Denver for reasons other than what you've said?" Clint asked.

Horn hesitated, then said, "I'm gonna confide in you, Adams, because I don't see any reason for you to turn around and bite me on the ass."

"I hope not," Clint said, "and if you're going to confide in me, you might as well call me Clint."

"Well, Clint," Horn said, "I'm sort of here on an undercover job."

"Undercover?" Clint asked. "So who are you really working for?"

"The Wyoming Stock Growers' Association."

"Wyoming?" Clint asked. "Why would you be undercover in Colorado?"

"The people in Wyoming are talkin' about starting another association, one that would link all the associations from other states and territories."

"Sounds like we're talking about powerful people," Clint said. "Rich ranchers like Zachary Green?"

"The people I work for are not so sure about Green," Horn said. "They have some questions about the way he runs his business. See, once they decide to move on this new organization, the first of the other associations they're gonna approach is Colorado."

"So you're here to feel Green out, see if he's on the up-and-up."

"That's right."

"So in order to do that," Clint said, "to get close enough, you had to work for him."

"Yep."

"But Roper was working for him."

"Now you're gettin' it."

"Wait a minute," Clint said. "Are you trying to tell me that you think somebody in the Wyoming Stock Growers' Association framed Roper for murder so that you could replace him in Zachary Green's employ?"

"I ain't sayin' I know that for a fact," Horn said. "I'm just sayin' it wouldn't surprise me."

"Well, it would surprise the hell out of me," Clint said with feeling. "They'd actually kill a woman and frame an innocent man to get their way?"

"Like you said," Horn replied, "they're rich, powerful people. People like that think they can do anything as long as they can pay for it."

"And you work for them?"

"Hey, they pay me a lot of money," Horn said. "I've got to earn a livin' too."

"Well, seems to me folks like that would turn on you quicker than a snake," Clint said. "If I was you, I'd be watching my step now and in the future."

"I think I can handle it." Horn reined in his horse. "This is as far as I go for now. If you need any help gettin' Roper out, just let me know."

"How do you mean?" Clint asked. "Breaking him out?"

."Whatever you say."

"Why would you help me break him out?"

Horn smiled and asked, "Why not?" and rode off back toward the Green ranch.

TWENTY-TWO

When Clint returned the rented horse to the Denver House stable, the poor animal was worn out.

"You better get yourself some new stock if this was the best you had," Clint said to the man.

"Yes, sir."

Clint entered the hotel through the back door and found himself being hailed by Justin, the desk clerk, as he went by.

"Justin."

"There was a policeman here looking for you a little while ago, Mr. Adams."

"What did you tell him?"

"I didn't tell him anything!" the man insisted. Then he calmed down and added, "I wasn't here when you left, so I didn't really know where you had gone."

"What was his name?"

"He left you a message."

Justin turned, retrieved the message from Clint's pigeonhole, and handed it to him.

"Thanks."

Clint decided to read it over a drink, so he went into the

hotel bar and ordered a beer from Mitch, the bartender. He managed to collect it and retreat to a table without exchanging any conversation, which suited him just fine.

He sat down and opened the envelope. The message was brief, which was just as well, because it was difficult to decipher the policeman's scrawl.

"Would like to talk with you. Will call again."

It was signed "Lieutenant Frank Pitt." Clint had dealt with some Denver policemen in the past but had never crossed paths with Lieutenant Pitt.

He refolded the message, put it back in the envelope, and tucked it away in his shirt pocket. He wondered when the lieutenant would be calling again; he got his answer much sooner than he would have imagined when a man entered the bar and looked around. He had "lawman" written all over him. Clint guessed that the lieutenant must have left a man in the lobby to watch for him. He'd certainly wasted no time in getting here.

Clint decided not to help the man out by waving. The man's suit was clean, though not expensive, and the bowler hat looked a bit out of place because he looked so young. He stopped and spoke with Mitch, who used his chin to point out Clint. As the man approached him, Clint realized he was not as young as he had first appeared, mid-thirties rather than late twenties. The lines around his eyes had not been visible from across the room.

The man removed his bowler and asked, "Clint Adams?"

"That's right."

"I'm Lieutenant Frank Pitt," he said. "I left a message for you at the front desk?"

Clint took the envelope out of his pocket and set it on the table, tapping it with his fingertips.

"I just read it," Clint said. "What a coincidence that you would call again just now."

"Not so much a coincidence," the lieutenant said. "I had a man in the lobby keeping an eye out for you. Do you mind if I sit down?"

"Not at all." Clint appreciated the man's candor. "Can I get you a beer?"

"I don't really drink when I'm on duty," Pitt said. He sat across from Clint and placed his hat on the table, but off to the right.

"What's this about, Lieutenant?"

"Talbot Roper."

"How do you mean?"

"It's my case," Pitt said. "I understand that you and he are friends?"

"That's right."

"And you're working for Wilson Perry?"

"Right again."

"I understand you desire to clear your friend, Mr. Adams," Pitt said. "I'm just hoping you won't be using your reputation to do it."

Clint sat back and regarded the lieutenant soberly.

"I'm not sure I understand what you're getting at, Lieutenant."

"I'm not trying to insult you, Mr. Adams," Pitt said. "I was just hoping you wouldn't be using any sort of . . . coercion to get what you wanted."

"First of all," Clint said, "if all you know about me is my reputation, Lieutenant, then you know nothing about me. Second, I'll probably use whatever methods I feel are necessary to prove Talbot Roper innocent of the charges against him."

"I'm sorry to hear that," the policeman said, "because he's guilty, so the only way you can prove him innocent is by some sort of . . . subterfuge."

"I guess we'll just have to wait and see then, won't we?"

"I suppose so."

"Then is there anything else I can do for you, Lieutenant?"

"I suppose not," Pitt said. He picked up his bowler hat. "Just know that I won't stand for any shenanigans from you."

"You're not from the West, are you, Lieutenant?"

"No," the man said, "I came from the East several years ago. I thought I had successfully blended in, though."

"Oh, I don't think you've been anywhere near as successful as you think."

"Why not?"

"No Westerner would ever use the word 'shenanigans.' "

TWENTY-THREE

It was with some relief that Ted Lanigan saw Clint Adams walking through the hotel lobby. He'd been so desperate to spot him that he had simply sat himself down in the lobby and waited. Now that Adams was there, Lanigan tried to fade into the background. He knew that if he got up to leave the man would see him. He had to stay where he was and hope he went unnoticed.

He watched Clint stop at the desk, and then felt relief again as he watched him cross the lobby and enter the bar. That was his chance to get up and leave. He was just about to do so when a man he recognized came through the front door. Once again, he tried to blend into the background as Lieutenant Pitt walked past him to the desk. While Pitt was talking at the front desk, Lanigan got up quickly and hurried to the front door and out of the hotel.

Outside, he breathed the fresh air and wondered what to do next. Wait for the policeman to leave? Wait for Adams to go to bed? And what was he going to tell his boss about what he'd done all day? Could he come up with a convincing lie, so he wouldn't have to admit that he'd lost Adams?

And if he did admit it, would Mike Brockton kill him in a fit of rage?

Clint would have liked to talk with Wilson Perry, but at this time of the evening the man wouldn't have been in his office, and Clint didn't know where he lived. He was stuck in his hotel, for want of anywhere else to go, so he decided to go to his room and go over the new files—the master files—that Jane Hutchinson had given him.

On the way to his room, he stopped at the desk and asked them to send up a pot of coffee.

"Of course, sir," Justin said. "I'll have that taken care of. Uh, one cup, or two?"

"Just one, Justin," Clint said. "I can only drink out of one cup at a time."

"Sorry, sir," Justin said, "I thought . . ."

"You thought what?"

"Well . . . just that you might be having company."

"I'm not," Clint said, "not that I know of anyway." In the past women had bribed their way into Clint's room, and although he mostly didn't mind, he gave Justin a hard stare and asked, "You haven't let anyone into my room, have you?"

"No, sir!" Justin said. "That would get me fired for sure."

"All right, Justin. Get that coffee sent up."

"Yes, sir."

Clint went to his room, turned up the wall lamp, then one that was sitting on a table by a chair. He was halfway through the first file when there was a knock on the door. He was surprised when he opened it to find Elizabeth Hannibal standing there with his coffee.

"This is getting to be a habit," he said, stepping back to let her in.

"I can't stay," she said, setting the tray with the coffee

and the cup on the table next to the chair. "I just wanted to come up to say . . . well, I just wanted to come up."

"Is there something you wanted to talk about?"

She turned and looked at him. "There's a rumor around the hotel about you and me . . . last night . . ."

"Well," he said, "that might explain Justin's reaction when I asked for coffee."

"Which was?"

"One cup or two?"

"Oh."

"If Mitch heard anything, though, he managed to control himself when I was in the bar."

"Mitch and Justin," she said. "They are not very happy to be working for a woman."

"And what about Sykes?"

"I don't think he knows yet."

"And when he does? Will he fire you?"

"Only if he can prove that I spent the night here."

"And can he?"

"No," she said. "Not unless you or I tell him."

"I won't."

"Neither will I," she said. "I just wanted you to know."

She started for the door.

"Elizabeth—"

She held her hand out to him.

"I'm not sorry about anything, Clint," she told him, "but I need to think for a while."

"All right."

She left. He was sorry she might be in trouble, but if she didn't want to see him again it would be okay. Neither of them had formed an emotional attachment after just one night.

Still, he wondered who had spread the rumor that they'd been together. Justin? Or Mitch Cannon?

He poured himself a cup of coffee before it could get

cold. He sat back down to go through the files again, but he wasn't finding all that much difference between the first master file and the corresponding one he had. Maybe a discrepancy would be more obvious in the second and third files.

TWENTY-FOUR

Clint woke the next morning, eyes bleary from reading over the files. From what he could see, there had been some names and addresses missing from the ones he'd gotten from Hutch. Had she been trying to hide these people from him?

He walked to the window and looked out. He knew Ted Lanigan, Brockton's man, could not have followed him yesterday, but he'd seen him in the lobby last night. He also wondered if Lanigan had admitted to his boss that he'd lost him.

Dressing, he thought briefly about Elizabeth Hannibal. Although the sheets on his bed had been changed by a maid, he could still smell Elizabeth in the room. He hoped that she would be able to handle the problem with the rumor. He didn't want to be the cause of her losing her job. He hoped that their night together would not end up being a bad memory for her.

He went down to the lobby and decided not to have breakfast in the hotel, but at a small restaurant he knew of down the street—if it was still there.

As he stepped outside, he looked around again, across the street, up and down the block, but did not catch sight of

Ted Lanigan. Since he already knew that the man was not that good at what he was doing, he could only conclude that the man simply was not there this morning.

He turned and headed off down the street.

Lieutenant Frank Pitt walked down to the water's edge, where the body was lying facedown in the Mississippi.

"Turn him over," he said to one of the uniformed men. "I want to see his face."

One of the men leaned over and obliged. Water dripped from the dead man's slack face.

"Know him, sir?" the policeman asked.

"Yes," Pitt said. "One of Mike Brockton's men. His name was Ted Lanigan. You can let him go now."

The policeman released the body, which fell facedown into the mud again.

"Wonder if Harvey Steelgrave had anything to do with this," the other policeman said.

"I doubt it," Pitt said.

"Why's that?"

"Lanigan is small potatoes," the Lieutenant said. "Steelgrave wouldn't bother." He leaned over again. "Two bullets in the back?"

"That's the way it looks," the first policeman said.

"All right," Pitt said, "get the body out of here."

He turned and walked back up the slope, the mud sucking at his shoes as he went.

Clint ate a leisurely breakfast and then headed back to the hotel. He'd been pleased to find the small restaurant still there since his last trip. It was good to have an alternative.

As he entered the lobby, he saw Lieutenant Frank Pitt waiting for him. The man's arms were crossed and he looked impatient.

"What did you do last night after I left?" he demanded of Clint without preamble.

"I went to my room."

"You didn't leave?"

"No."

"Can anybody testify to that?"

There was Elizabeth, but Clint didn't want Pitt to know that she had come to his room.

"No," he said. "What's this about?"

"You know a man named Lanigan? Ted Lanigan?"

"No, I don't."

"He was in the lobby last night when I got here," Pitt said. "Doing his best to be invisible, but he's not very good at it."

"I knew somebody was watching me," Clint said. "Is that what you're getting at?"

"Exactly," Pitt said. "You didn't confront him?"

"No," Clint said, "I just made it a little difficult for him."

"You lost him?"

"Yes."

"His boss wouldn't like that very much."

"His boss?"

"A man named Mike Brockton. Do you know him?"

"No, but I've heard the name," Clint admitted. "What's this all about, Lieutenant?"

"We found Lanigan facedown in the river this morning, with two bullets in his back."

"And you thought I did it?" Clint asked. "I've never shot anybody in the back in my life. If I kill a man, he's facing me."

"What is that, some kind of code?"

"A very personal one."

"I can't prove you had anything to do with his death," Pitt said, "but I do think his death has something to do with you."

"I hope you're wrong," Clint said. "I'd hate to be the cause of someone's death—unless I pull the trigger myself."

"You like killing men who are facing you?"

"Let's just say if I kill a man, it's usually because he's trying to kill me."

"Well, that wouldn't be Lanigan," Pitt said. "He was strictly small-time. Brockton used him for errands."

"Then maybe he got killed while running another errand."

"Or maybe because he messed up this one," Pitt said.

"I wish you luck finding out."

"Yes, well, I better get to it."

Pitt turned to leave, then stopped and turned back.

"Tell me something, Mr. Adams."

"What?"

"When you lost Lanigan, where did you go?"

"I went for a ride, Lieutenant," Clint said. "If you check with the stable here, you'll find out I rented a horse and went for a ride."

"To anywhere in particular?"

"No," Clint said. "I just needed to have a horse underneath me again for a few hours."

"You wouldn't tell me the truth no matter what I asked you, would you?"

"On the contrary," Clint said, "I have told you the truth."

Most of the time, he thought as Pitt turned and left.

TWENTY-FIVE

Clint went to Wilson Perry's office and was lucky enough to catch the man in.

"I've got court in twenty minutes," Perry said, "so we'll have to make it fast."

Clint told the lawyer about his talk with Zachary Green, and then about his discussion with Tom Horn.

"I know Horn by reputation," Perry said, loading some papers into a leather case while he spoke. "I wouldn't put too much credence in what he has to say."

"You only know me by reputation too, Wilson," Clint said.

Perry stopped stuffing the papers into his leather case and looked at Clint.

"Can I be honest?"

"Please."

"I wasn't too sure about you either, Clint, but Roper insisted on having you clear him."

"And now?"

"Since I've met you and we've talked, I'm inclined to believe less about your reputation," Perry said. "I thought you'd be this wild and woolly gunman, but I see you're not."

"Well, from what I can tell," Clint said, "neither is Horn."

"Do you really think that reputable cattlemen like the men who run the Wyoming Association would kill a woman and frame an innocent man to further their goals?"

"If it meant making more money for themselves," Clint said, "hell, yes."

Perry thought a moment, then said, "Okay, you have a point. What do you intend to do now?"

"Talk to some more of the people involved with Roper's cases," Clint said. "That's all I can do."

"All right," Perry said. He finished packing his leather case, picked it up, and cradled it under his arm. "Continue to keep me informed."

"I will."

They left the building together. Outside, Clint put his hand on Perry's arm. "One more thing."

"What's that?"

He told Perry about Ted Lanigan being found dead that morning, and that the police might suspect him.

"Who spoke with you? Lieutenant Pitt?"

"That's the man."

"Pitt's a zealot," Perry said. "Ever since he made lieutenant, he thinks he can close down all the crime in Denver. His main targets are Harvey Steelgrave and Mike Brockton, and he'll do anything he has to do to get them."

"Why is he so intent in getting Roper then?"

"If you can believe it," Perry said, "he actually thinks Roper is guilty. He has no other agenda that I can see."

"So he's honest?"

"As honest as they come."

Perry waved and got into his carriage without offering Clint a lift.

TWENTY-SIX

Mike Brockton was still livid, even though it had been hours since he'd pumped two bullets into Ted Lanigan's back as the man was leaving his office. Lanigan had tried lying, but Brockton had seen right through him. Did he really think Brockton was going to just let him walk out?

The door to his office opened and Bill Jory walked in. Jory was Brockton's right-hand man. They had hit town at the same time, met and liked each other, and the rest was Denver crime history. Jory had been standing right there when Brockton plugged Lanigan and hadn't even blinked.

"Well?"

"The police found him already," Jory said.

"Where'd you dump him?"

"Down by the river."

"Not in the river?"

"No."

"Why not?"

Jory shrugged. "He'd just wash up anyway," he said. "This way it gives Pitt something else to concentrate on."

"That little . . . Is he the one who's been talking to Clint Adams?"

"Yes."

Brockton smiled. "He probably thinks Adams did it, since Lanigan was keeping watch on him."

"Probably."

"What about Roper?"

"Still inside," Jory said. "Still looks good for the murder of the woman."

"We got anybody inside?"

"A couple of people."

Brockton rubbed his jaw. "Put the word out," he said. "If Roper doesn't make it to trial, I won't be unhappy."

"Okay."

"Get it done quick."

"Today quick enough?"

Brockton smiled again. He knew he could always count on Jory to do what he was told.

"Today would be perfect."

Jory nodded and left the room.

Within hours Talbot Roper was attacked while working in the prison laundry. He sensed something behind him as he was washing some sheets and pillowcases by hand, and turned just at the right moment. Two men had moved up behind him, both with knives. He whipped a wet sheet at them, causing them to dodge. Instead of charging them, though, he turned to get away from them. He needed to put some distance between him and them until he could find a weapon.

As he slid away, he deliberately upset the tun of soapy water he'd been using. Both men slipped on the water, only one going down on his ass. The other one regained his balance and went after Roper.

The three men were alone in the room. If Roper hadn't been moping—and he'd been doing that too much since they put him in jail—he would have noticed that other prisoners had left the room. Nobody wanted to witness what was going to happen.

He looked for a weapon, but there was nothing he could really use—not against two big men with knives. The other man had righted himself, and now the two of them were advancing on him as he found himself with his back to the wall. He didn't know what gleamed more, the glint in their eyes or the light off their blades. He noticed that the knives were not homemade, so they must have been smuggled in somehow. The men were about to eviscerate him, and someone had put them up to it.

He'd just about decided to rush them and try to do some damage before they killed him when something grabbed them from behind. It stopped their forward progress, and suddenly they were propelled backward, their eyes wide with surprise.

Roper hadn't seen Butch Brooks come up behind them because Brooks was short. He was wide, though, and powerfully built, but he wasn't as wide as the two men standing side by side, so Roper had found out about his presence at the same time the two men had.

He watched as Butch took one of their arms and broke it in half with an audible crack. He then turned to the other man, who tried to swipe at him with the knife. That made Butch mad, so he not only snapped the man's forearm, but his wrist as well. Both knives clattered to the ground and the two men began to howl.

"Thanks, Butch," Roper said, stepping forward.

Brooks turned and stared at him with dead eyes.

"Didn't do it for you."

"Why'd you help me then?" Roper asked.

"They work for Brockton," Butch Brooks said. "I'm a Steelgrave man. That was good enough reason for me."

"Well," Roper said, "whatever the reason, thanks."

"Guards'll be here soon," Brooks said. "You gonna back my play, Roper?"

"No problem, Butch," Roper said. "I got your back from now on."

TWENTY-SEVEN

Clint went to see Roper. As promised by Wilson Perry, he got in with no problem. All the guards did was disarm him.

"You'll get it back when you leave," said one of the guards.

Clint nodded, and they admitted him to the interview room to await Roper. The same guard brought him in, gave him the same push.

"You're a lucky man, Roper," the guard said.

Clint turned to the surly guard and said, "Do you mind waiting outside?"

The guard hesitated, then said, "Sure," and left, closing the door behind him.

"What's he mean, you're a lucky man?" Clint asked as Roper sat across from him.

"Two of Mike Brockton's men tried to kill me earlier today," Roper said.

"How did that go?"

"Two big men, two big knives."

"What happened?"

"A bigger man with no knife, but he's mean."

"Somebody helped you?"

"Saved me is more like it," Roper said. "His name is Butch Brooks. He worked for Steelgrave."

"Ah."

"He snapped their arms like twigs."

"Does he like you or something?"

"No," Roper said, then, "No, nothing like that. No, he said it was enough that he's a Steelgrave man and they were Brockton men. He was happy to do it."

"What'd they do to him?" Clint asked. "The prison guards, I mean. Did he get in trouble?"

"No," Roper said. "They didn't do anything to him. I told them the two guys jumped him."

"Must make the two of you buddies now."

"Not really."

"He helped you, you covered his back," Clint said. "That sounds close enough."

"Never mind," Roper said. "What have you got for me?"

Clint told Roper everything he'd done so far, and finished up with his conversation with Tom Horn.

"Do you know anyone in the Wyoming Stock Growers' Association?" Clint asked.

"As a matter of fact, I do. A man named Arthur England."

"Anything happen between you and England?"

"I refused to work for him."

"Why?"

Roper shrugged. "I didn't like him."

"How did he take that?"

"Personally."

"And when was that?"

"A couple of months ago."

"Would he do this to you because of that?"

Roper hesitated, then said, "I don't honestly know."

"What do you know about Lieutenant Frank Pitt?"

"Pitt," Roper said. "Honest, but to a fault."

"He's out to get you."

"At this point," Talbot Roper said, "I'm starting to feel like . . . who isn't?"

"I've still got a lot of people to talk to, Tal," Clint said, "but will I be wasting my time?"

"What do you mean?"

"Is it Brockton who's behind framing you?"

"If it was, why would he want me killed?"

"Then this fella England."

"I don't know," Roper said. "It could still be somebody connected to one of my cases."

"The banker, the outlaw, and the rancher," Clint said. "And now another rancher, England . . . and another outlaw, Brockton. The list is getting long."

"Don't forget the cop."

"I've got another question."

"What is it?"

"It's about your girl, Hutch."

"What about her?"

"She left some things out of the files she gave me."

"What things?"

"Some names and addresses."

Roper frowned. "Why would she do that?"

"I don't know," Clint said. "That's what I was going to ask you."

"Well," he said, "ask *her*."

Clint ran his hands over his face.

"Keep at it, Clint," Roper said. "Keep asking questions. Sooner or later, the answer will become clear."

"Is that how you do it?" Clint asked. "Just keep asking questions?"

"I don't want to simplify what I do too much," Roper said, "but that's what I do."

TWENTY-EIGHT

Clint left the jail, worried that somebody might try to kill Roper again. Roper told him not to worry, but that was easier said than done. Clint figured he'd better let Perry know what had happened in the jail. Maybe the lawyer could do something to keep Roper away from the rest of the prisoners.

Of course, as long as Roper had Butch Brooks watching his back . . . but how long could that go on?

Clint had left the files at his hotel and went back there to read them. He needed to add some names and addresses to the list Hutch had originally given him. When he got there, he found somebody waiting for him in the lobby. It was getting to be a habit.

"Hi," Hutch said.

"Hello."

"Can we talk?"

"In public or in private?" he asked.

"You could buy me a drink."

"To tell you the truth," he said, "I could use one myself."

Jory came into Brockton's office looking dissatisfied.

"Don't tell me," Brockton said. "Roper's not dead."

111

"No."

Brockton sighed and sat back in his chair.

"What happened?"

"You know a guy name Butch Brooks?"

"Yeah," Brockton said. "He works for Steelgrave."

"He took our two men apart just as they were about to kill Roper," Jory said. "I don't know why. He and Roper weren't close then—"

"It's enough that they were my men," Brockton said. "What do you mean, they weren't close then?"

"Well, Brooks saved Roper, and Roper covered for Brooks," Jory said. "That kind of thing tends to form a bond."

"So what you're saying is that Roper and Brooks are watching each other's backs now."

"Right."

Brockton closed his eyes and shook his head.

"I mean," Jory said, "we could still get to Roper. It would just take a lot more men."

"No," Brockton said, "don't do anything. Let's just let it lie for now. Put out the word. Nobody touches Roper. It would attract too much attention."

"Okay. Sorry, Mike."

"Not your fault, Jory."

Jory didn't leave.

"Something else?"

"We haven't replaced Lanigan," Jory said. "Nobody's watching Adams, and there's no one on the girl."

"Lanigan messed this up real good, didn't he?" Brockton said. "I wish he was alive so I could kill him again."

Harvey Steelgrave looked up as Eddie the bartender walked into his office.

"What is it, Eddie?"

"Thought you might like to hear some news."

"News," Steelgrave asked, "or gossip?"

Eddie shrugged.

"Okay, give it to me."

Eddie told his boss about the "incident" in prison when two of Brockton's men had tried to kill Talbot Roper.

"Sounds like Butch is doin' his job," Steelgrave said.

"Yep."

"See that his wife gets some extra money this week, Eddie," Steelgrave said. "A lot extra."

"Okay."

"Is Stanton out there?"

"Yes."

"Tell him to come in."

"Okay."

"Leave the door open for him on your way out."

Eddie went out the door, and soon Romeo Stanton came walking in. Why his parents would have named him Romero thirty-two years ago Steelgrave didn't know, but he knew the man was touchy about being asked.

"Sit down, Romeo," Steelgrave said.

As touchy as he was, though, Stanton liked his first name. A man who could only be called ugly, he thought that name made him sound romantic. He thought that because as soon as he had learned how to read he'd read the play by Shakespeare. Maybe that was why his parents had named him that. Maybe one or both of them had liked the play, and the name.

"I've got a job for you."

"What is it?"

"I want you to keep somebody alive for me."

"Who?"

"His name's Clint Adams."

"The Gunsmith?" Stanton asked. "Why would he need somebody to keep him alive?"

"Well," Steelgrave said, "basically, because I say so."

Stanton shrugged. "Okay."

"What are you carrying?"

Stanton pulled his jacket back to reveal a .32 in a shoulder rig.

"Wear something with more firepower," Steelgrave said, "something that would give you more distance."

"Yeah, okay. When do I start?"

"Now," Steelgrave said. "Get yourself outfitted, and get over to the Denver House Hotel. Talk to Eddie. He'll tell you what the man looks like."

"Right."

Stanton got up to leave.

"Romeo."

"Yeah?" He stopped at the door.

"Don't worry about him seein' you."

Stanton frowned.

"And if he braces you," his boss went on, "just tell him why you're there."

"Tell him the truth?"

"I know it's not a concept you appreciate," Steelgrave said, "but yes, tell him the truth."

TWENTY-NINE

"What's this about, Hutch?" Clint asked.

They were seated at a table in the empty bar. It was early, and apparently no one else was drinking yet. The bartender—not Mitch—was busy cleaning glasses and was not paying attention to them.

Clint had a beer, and Hutch had a glass of brandy.

"It's about those files," she said.

"What about them?"

"I want to tell you why I left those names out."

"Okay, why?"

"I was told to."

"By who?"

"A man?"

"Do you know his name?"

"No."

"Who he worked for?"

"No."

"When was this?"

"After Mr. Roper was arrested."

"And why did you decide to do what this man told you to do?" Clint asked.

"He said if I did what he said, Mr. Roper would be safe in jail."

"Somebody tried to kill Roper today."

"I know," she said. "I heard."

"How did you hear that?"

"I know a girl who works at the jail," she said. "She knows that I work for Mr. Roper."

"So that's why you decided to come here and tell me this?"

"If someone has already tried to kill him, then that man is not keeping his word."

"You'd know the man if you saw him again, right?"

"Oh, yes."

"I may ask you to look at someone in the near future."

"Whatever you want," she said. "I—I don't want you to think badly of me. That's another reason I came to tell you."

"I see."

"Do you think Mr. Roper will fire me?" she asked. "For tampering with his files?"

"Under the circumstances," he said, "I don't think so."

"That's good."

She sat back in her chair, seemingly relieved. She looked around.

"I've never been here before," she said. "It's quite nice."

"Yes," he said, "it is."

"And I've never seen the rooms."

That was fairly obvious, he thought, if she'd never been there before. She sipped her drink and licked her lips. She was looking quite fetching today, her hair long and clean. He could smell whatever she'd used to clean it from across the table.

Then something occurred to him.

"Hutch, did the man tell you what names to leave out of the files?" he asked.

"He told me one," she said. "I left the others out to . . . to hide what I was doing."

"Do you remember the name he told you to leave out?"

"Yes."

"Which file was it in?"

She blinked at him and said, "Do you know? I can't remember that."

"The files are in my room," he said. "If you look at them, can you pick the name out?"

"Yes, I can."

"Do you mind coming to my room with me?"

She set her glass down very carefully, then licked her lips again, even though she hadn't taken a sip.

"Why, no, Clint, I don't mind at all."

THIRTY

Truth be told, he didn't expect to end up in bed with her when they went to his room.

Well, yeah, he did, but he never expected it to be her bed . . .

When they got to his room, he sat her down and showed her the master files she had given him.

"This one," she said, pointing to a name in one of the files.

"I better write down the name and the address," he said.

"Here, I'll do it for you."

She found a piece of paper in the file with just a few words on it, turned it over, and wrote down the name and address.

"Leave it in the file," he said, "so I don't forget which one it goes with."

She slid the paper into the file and then put the file down on the table next to the chair.

"This is a beautiful room," she said.

"Yes, it is," he said, "but I think you should be leaving."

"Why?" she asked.

He hesitated, trying to come up with a good reason,

then said, "I think it would be for the best. Besides, there must be work for you to do at the office."

She stared at him for a few moments, then stood up and smoothed the front of her dress, which drew his eyes. She was taller, more willowy than Elizabeth Hannibal, but looked to have perfectly rounded breasts. It wasn't easy to send her away, because he had the feeling she would be willing, and more than able.

"Would you walk me down?" she asked.

"Of course."

"Just let me sneak a peek into your bedroom," she said.

She walked to the door while he stayed where he was.

"Nice big bed." She turned her head and looked over her shoulder at him.

"Come on, Hutch," he said. "Time to go home."

She turned around and approached him.

"Don't you find me attractive?"

"Very."

"Then what's the problem?"

"I have too much respect for you to take advantage of you in my room."

She seemed about to say something, but thought better of it, turned, and walked to the door.

"Are you coming?" she asked.

When they got down to the lobby, he walked her to the front door.

"I'll leave you in the capable hands of the doorman. He'll get you a cab."

They walked to the front door and stepped outside. Immediately, Clint saw Ted Lanigan's replacement standing across the street.

"What is it?" Hutch asked.

"A bad man, I think."

"Where?" Her head swiveled from side to side.

"Across the street. Don't look."

She looked.

"Hutch."

"Is he watching me or you?"

"Me, I think."

"You'll have to take me home," she said.

"If you leave and he stays, we'll know he's watching me."

"And if I leave and he follows, what will you do?"

"Chase both of you."

"If you take me home and he follows you back, then we'll know he's watching you."

"All right," Clint said. "Doorman, a cab."

Clint saw the man grab a cab and follow them, which didn't tell them a thing. And the fact that he was in front of the hotel didn't tell him a thing either, because the man could have followed her there.

"Is he still there?" she asked.

"He's following."

"What does he want?"

"I don't know, Hutch," Clint said. "I guess I'll have to ask him." Considering what had happened with Ted Lanigan, Clint figured he'd better make contact with the man quickly, after taking Hutch home.

"Wait a minute," he said.

"What?"

"Why am I taking you home instead of to the office?"

"I'm nervous," she said. "When I get nervous I have to lie down. Besides, there really isn't that much work to do at the office without Mr. Roper there."

"All right," Clint said, "I'll drop you home, and then I'll see what this fella wants."

She slid her hand into his and held on tight, as if she was never going to let go.

THIRTY-ONE

Hutch dragged Clint into her rooms with her, refusing to let go of his hand.

"Just take me inside," she said. "Make sure I'm safe. The cab will wait for you."

"All right," he said, and told the driver to wait. The man gave him a leer he ignored.

Hutch used her key to unlock her door, then turned to Clint and said, "Would you check inside for me?"

"Sure."

He walked in, found himself in a small sitting room. Off to the left he could se a bed in another room, and to the right a small kitchen. When he turned to face her, she already had her dress down around her waist. He'd been right about her breasts. They were round and perfect, tipped with pink nipples.

"What do you think you're doing?" he asked.

When Romeo Stanton saw the man come out of the hotel with the pretty woman, he knew it was Clint Adams. Eddie the bartender's description had been perfect.

He watched as Adams and the woman got into a cab,

then went around the corner, where he had paid a cab driver to sit and wait until he needed him.

"All day?" the man had asked.

"All day," Stanton had said, giving him some money. "Same again at the end of the day."

"Fine with me." The driver tipped his hat down over his eyes and went to sleep.

But he was awake as soon as Romeo touched his shoulder.

"Follow that cab."

When they reached their destination, he watched as the woman seemingly had to drag Clint Adams into her home.

"She wouldn't have to drag me," the driver said.

"Me neither," Stanton said.

"So what do we do now?" the driver asked.

"He's got his driver waitin'," Stanton said. "We'll wait too."

"Fine with me," the man said. He tipped his hat down over his eyes and went to sleep.

"You said you didn't want to take advantage of me in your room," she reminded him. "Well, these are my rooms."

"Hutch—"

"I'm not the silly woman I seem to be, Clint," she told him. "That's an act."

"Why the act?" He had thought once or twice that she was acting too young for her age.

"Men expect it," she said. "I find it to my advantage sometimes to give men what they expect."

She pushed at her dress and it fell down to her ankles. Next, she slithered out of her underwear and it followed. She stepped from the heap of clothes and approached him. He thought he could feel the heat of her body through his own clothes.

"You said you found me attractive."

"I do," Clint said, his mouth feeling dry, "but I've got work to do, Hutch—"

She pressed her naked body tightly up against him and said, "Then let's get to this fast. I don't mind fast, Clint. Fast and hard."

What was it with the women of Denver? he wondered. First Elizabeth and now Hutch, fast and hard.

Well, he thought, if she found it to her advantage to give men what they wanted, maybe he'd have an advantage if he gave her what she wanted.

He reached around to cup her smooth buttocks, and kissed her on the mouth, which immediately opened beneath his. Her tongue was a hot, slithering thing, darting into his mouth as she slid a hand down to cup his crotch.

He pushed her away then.

"Wha—"

He took her by the shoulders, turned her so that her back was to her bedroom, then walked her into the room that way. Once they were inside, he pushed her again, hard. She fell onto the bed, her hair falling across her eyes.

"What are you doing?" she gasped.

He was shucking his clothes as quickly as possible, because suddenly he was very excited.

"Hard and fast, you said."

"Yes, bu—"

"I'm going to give you what you want, Hutch."

His gun belt hit the floor with his trousers and underwear. He advanced on her, his erection wagging in front of him like a diving rod going right for her wetness.

He shoved her onto her back, mounted her, and brutally entered her.

"Oh, yessss . . ." she hissed.

THIRTY-TWO

Clint slid his cock in and out of Hutch as she writhed beneath him. She was slick and wet, and had a sharp, almost tangy smell down there that he found intoxicating. He'd meant to fuck her hard and get out of there, to sort of teach her a lesson, but instead he withdrew from her and then slithered down to replace his cock with his mouth.

"Ohhh, God," she said, "what are you—oh!"

He licked her up and down, then found her rigid clit and began to flick it with the tip of his tongue. After that, he circled it with pursed lips and drew it between them. At the same time he reached up, squeezed her breasts, pinched her nipples until she had to bite her lip to keep from screaming. She began to wriggle her butt, so he slid his hands beneath her cheeks to cup them and lifted her to his mouth as he continued to avidly eat her.

"Oh, Clint, Jesus," she said, reaching for him, "you're killing meeeeee . . . don't stop. . . ."

He had no intention of stopping, but he wanted her in a different way now. He had a new plan to teach her a lesson, and that was to take her in every possible way.

He flipped her over onto her belly, slapped her butt hard, leaving a red mark on her right cheek, then grabbed

her hips, lifted her, and entered her vagina from behind. He
fucked her that way until he was good and wet from her
sweet slime, then withdrew, parted her ass cheeks, and entered her that way.

"Oooh . . . oohhh . . . wha—Jeez, I never . . . oooohh . . ."
She couldn't talk but could only make unintelligible sounds
at this point as he took her that way. His belly slapped into
her ass cheeks and filled the air with the sound of flesh
meeting flesh. She was tight, and he grunted as he continued to fuck her. She got to her knees and started slamming
herself back into him, meeting him thrust for thrust. She
supported herself on one hand and reached out to grab the
bedpost with the other.

While he fucked her from behind, he reached around to
touch her with his hand, sliding a finger into her and then
up over her engorged clit. She went wild when he did that,
began to slam into him more violently, the bed moving beneath them, actually jumping across the room inch by inch.
He was about to explode inside her when suddenly the
door flew open in the other room and he immediately be-
came aware of men pouring into the place.

The only thing that saved him is that he and Hutch were
in the bedroom. He had time to pull clear of Hutch and grab
his gun from the floor, where he'd foolishly allowed it to fall.

He turned then as four men hit the bedroom doorway.
Again, an oddity saved him as the four men tried to get into
the room at the same time. He fired once, then again, heard
grunts of pain from someone—maybe two someones, if he
was lucky.

Naked, Clint backed his way across the floor on both
feet and one hand, like a three-legged spider. He kept his
other hand outstretched, pointing the gun at the doorway,
preparing to fire again. Suddenly, he heard shots, but they
weren't coming from the men, but seemed to be coming
from behind them. . . .

•   •   •

Romeo Stanton had noticed when the four men appeared at the front door of the woman's rooms. One of them seemed to insert a key into the lock, and then they drew their guns, opened the door, and flooded inside.

"Shit," he said, and started running across the street, his own gun out.

Clint fired again and the four men, caught in a cross fire somehow, all hit the floor, dead. When they weren't blocking the doorway, he saw a man in the other room holding a gun. Clint held his fire, because the man seemed to have helped him.

"What the—" he said, then saw the man turn his gun toward the bed. "No!" he shouted, but he was too late. The man fired once and Jane Hutchinson hit the floor, also dead. She was lying half on and half off the bed, her legs still on it, her butt in the air.

"Jesus," Clint said. "What the hell did you do that for?"

The man entered the room, approached the bed, leaned over, and took a small .32-caliber pistol from the dead woman's hand.

"She was gonna shoot you in the back."

"Wha—"

"You was set up," Romeo Stanton said.

"Who are you?" Clint asked.

"Romeo."

"You're the man following me?"

Stanton nodded.

"I saw them come in," he said. "They used a key."

"A key?" Clint was still feeling confused. It seemed Talbot Roper's secretary had set him up to be killed.

But for God's sake, why?

Obviously, he wasn't going to get any answers from her.

"You better get dressed," Romeo said. "The police will be here soon."

With that, he turned and left.

THIRTY-THREE

"And you don't know the man who helped you?" Lieutenant Frank Pitt asked.

"Never saw him before."

"Do you have any idea who he might be?"

"Not a clue."

"How about who he works for?"

"Couldn't tell you."

"What about the other four?"

"Never saw them before."

"Are you sure?"

"I'm positive."

"Did you get a good look at them?"

"I did," Clint said, "after they were dead."

They were in Pitt's office at the Denver Police Headquarters Building. Uniformed police had responded to the shooting at Jane Hutchinson's house. Clint could not figure out what had happened with her, why she'd suddenly turned. Could it be she'd been planted in Roper's office right from the beginning? Roper was going to be embarrassed if that was the case, because he'd never been taken in by a woman before—or at least, had never admitted to it.

"What about the woman?" Pitt asked.

"What about her?"

"What's her story?" Pitt asked. "She worked for Talbot Roper, right?"

"Supposedly."

"So why do you think she turned on you?"

"I don't know," Clint said. "Money?"

"She was naked when my men arrived."

"Yes."

"With one bullet in her chest."

"If you say so."

Pitt sat back in his chair.

"I'm not happy with the way this conversation is going, Adams," he said.

"To tell you the truth, Lieutenant, I'm not happy with the way the day is going," Clint said. "I don't like being taken in by a woman. It's not good for my self-esteem."

"Well, if she took you in, she probably also fooled Roper."

"And he's not going to be happy about that either."

"True," Pitt said thoughtfully. "I guess I should tell him."

"I can tell him—"

"No," Pitt said, "I think I'd rather do it."

"Then can I go?"

"You can go," Pitt said.

"Can I have my gun?"

"No."

"What?"

"You killed some men with it," Pitt said. "I'm going to hang onto it until I find out who they were."

"They were trying to kill me."

"No gun, Adams," Pitt said. "You can go, and I hate saying this, but don't leave Denver. I'm not finished with you yet."

"Don't worry," Clint said. "I'm not finished here by a long shot either."

•   •   •

Outside, Clint hailed a cab right away and told the man to get him to the Denver House Hotel fast. He didn't like being on the street without a gun.

When he got to the hotel, he hurried to his room and dug out the only other gun he had with him, other than a rifle, and that was his little Colt New Line. He wished he had something bigger, with more firepower. He was going to have to either go out and buy something, or go to Roper's office and see what was there. He decided to go to the office first.

He left the hotel only moments after he arrived. He looked around but could not see his benefactor anywhere. The man hadn't been hiding before, so the fact that he couldn't see him now led Clint to believe he wasn't there.

He was probably reporting back to whoever he worked for, and Clint had an idea who that might be. He was going to check it out, but first he had to come up with a bigger, more powerful gun.

Romeo entered Steelgrave's office and stood in front of his desk.

"What are you doing here?" Steelgrave asked. "You're supposed to be watching Adams."

"I will be," Stanton said. "I wanted to report in."

"About what?"

Stanton told Steelgrave about the four men who had tried to kill Clint Adams.

"Four men," he said, "and a woman."

"The woman?" Steelgrave asked. "The one who worked for Tal Roper?"

"Yes."

"And you killed her?"

"Yes," Stanton said, "to save Adams. You told me to make sure he wasn't harmed."

"Yes, I did," Steelgrave said. "And you did a good job. Can you pick him up again?"

"Yes," Stanton said, "no problem."

"Something's bothering me, Romeo."

"What's that, Boss?"

"The woman," Steelgrave said. "For the amount of time I was having her watched, she gave no indication of working for anyone else."

"You want me to find out who?"

"How would you do that?"

Stanton shrugged. "Ask around."

"You can do that and guard Adams?"

"We'll find out," Stanton said. "Or you can have someone else do it, if you like. Either way I get paid, right?"

"Oh, you get paid all right," Steelgrave said. "Just keep doin' your job the way you're doin' it."

"Should I ask around?"

"Okay."

But as he started to leave, Steelgrave called him back.

"Romeo."

"Yeah?"

"Did you recognize any of the four men?"

"I only saw them from across the street."

"What about when you were killing them?"

"Then I saw their guns."

"And after that?"

"I got out of there before the police got there."

"So you don't know if they worked for Brockton."

"No, sir," Romeo said. "But that would be my guess. Wouldn't it be yours?"

"Oh, yeah," Steelgrave said, "and if it is Brockton, he's tried to have Roper killed, and Adams."

"Probably won't stop there," Stanton said. "I gotta go, Boss. I'll let you know what I find out."

"Go," Steelgrave said. "Send Eddie in on your way out."

"Right."

Clint stopped at Roper's office, forced the front door, and let himself in. Jane Hutchinson's desk was neat and clean.

He went into Roper's office and started going through his desk drawers. He found what he wanted in one of the bottom drawers. It was an old Navy Colt, one of the largest handguns ever made. He didn't know why Roper had it, but it was in working order, and it was loaded. In addition, there were some extra bullets rolling around in the drawer. He took them out and pocketed them, then tucked the Navy Colt into the front of his belt. The New Line was snug at the small of his back.

He left the office and headed for the docks.

THIRTY-FOUR

As Romeo Stanton was leaving the River's Edge, he saw Clint Adams walking purposefully toward the place. He went back inside, crossed the room, and went out the side door just as Clint entered the front. He kept the door ajar so he could watch.

Clint entered the River's Edge, saw that Eddie the bartender was not behind the bar, and walked directly to the door in the back that led to Steelgrave's office.

"Hey," a man called out, "ya can't go in—" But he ignored him and opened the door.

Eddie was standing in front of Steelgrave's desk and turned as he heard the door open.

"Mr. Adams," Steelgrave said. "What a pleasant surprise. Eddie, out."

"Okay, Boss."

Eddie gave Clint a look as he went by, but was ignored. He left, closing the door behind him.

"What can I do for you?" Steelgrave asked.

"You've had a man watching me."

"Have I?"

"Big fella, good with a gun. I'm not here to complain. He saved my life."

"So I heard."

"From who?"

"From him," Steelgrave said. "His name's Romeo."

"Romeo?"

"Stanton," Steelgrave said with a nod.

"Why did you have him watching me?"

"So he could save your life."

"Why?"

"So you can save Roper's life."

"Why do you want Roper saved? And don't tell me because he's a good detective."

"Okay," Steelgrave said, "I won't."

Clint waited for something else to be offered, but nothing was coming.

"What about the other man?"

"What other man?"

"The one who was killed," Clint said. "The other one who was watching me."

Steelgrave shook his head. "Romeo's the first man I put on you."

"Is that the truth?"

"Yes," Steelgrave said. "I told you before, the other man worked for Brockton. In fact, Brockton probably had him killed, or killed him himself."

"Why would he kill his own man?"

"Maybe he failed him."

Clint rubbed his jaw. "He did lose me."

"That would do it," Steelgrave said. "Brockton has killed more of his own men in a fit of rage . . . if I just wait, he'll probably wipe out his own men completely. What is that in your belt?"

"A Navy Colt."

"Where's your gun?"

"The police kept it."

"Pitt?"

"Yes."

"Where'd you get that?"

"From Roper's office."

"Do you want something else?"

"No," Clint said, "this is fine. I examined it. It's in working order, and it has the stopping power I want."

"You need a holster for it," Steelgrave said.

"Well . . . yeah."

"Let me see what I've got."

Steelgrave stood up, turned, and walked to a wooden cabinet set against the back wall. As he opened it, Clint saw that it was a gun cabinet. He saw two Winchesters, a Greener shotgun, a Remington. . . . Steelgrave opened a drawer, took out a holster, withdrew the gun from it, and set that back in the drawer before closing it.

Before closing the cabinet, he asked, "You want a shotgun?"

"Not right now."

Steelgrave closed the cabinet and returned to his desk. Instead of sitting, he extended the holster to Clint. It wasn't new, but the leather had been oiled and well cared for.

"I think that'll fit."

Clint took the Navy Colt from his belt, fitted it into the holster, then strapped the holster on.

"You change your mind about that shotgun, let me know."

"I'll keep the offer in mind. What about your man, Romeo?"

"He's still going to be watching your back," Steelgrave said. "That is, unless you want him next to you?"

"No," Clint said, "having him behind me is okay for now."

"He's a good man."

"I don't doubt it."

"You getting' any closer to findin' out who framed Roper?"

"Somebody tried really hard to kill me today," Clint said on his way out, "so it would seem so."

THIRTY-FIVE

Clint stopped at the bar and told Eddie to give him a beer.

"Where's Romeo?" Clint asked.

"Uh, what?"

"Come on, Eddie," Clint said. "Steelgrave told me Romeo's been watching my back, and earlier today he saved my life. I want to buy him a beer."

Eddie was a bad liar, because as he said, "I don't know where he is," his eyes slid off to the side. Clint assumed there was a back or side door somewhere.

"Why don't you just bring him over and I'll buy him a beer?" Clint asked.

"I don't know—"

"For Chrissake, Eddie," Clint said. "Ask Steelgrave if you want, but just do it."

Eddie moved out from behind the bar, and Clint stared into his beer. He could feel the eyes of the other men in the place on his back, but he doubted anyone was going to approach him. He straightened and shifted the strange holster on his hips. Strange holster, strange gun. It certainly wasn't an ideal situation with people out there trying to kill him.

When Eddie returned, he brought with him the big man Clint had seen in Jane Hutchinson's rooms.

"Romeo?" he asked.

"That's right."

Clint looked at Eddie, who hurriedly placed a beer mug in front of Romeo Stanton.

"I wanted to thank you for what you did," Clint said.

"I was doing my job."

"Anyway . . . have a beer."

"Thanks."

They both took time to sip some of their beer. Clint put his down after a sip, but Romeo drank down half of his.

"I'm sorry you had to kill the woman."

The other man shrugged. "Part of the job."

"It doesn't bother you?"

"No."

"Well, let me ask you . . . are you sure she was in on it?"

"You sayin' I was wrong to kill her?" Romeo asked. "She was pointing a gun at your back."

Clint's back began to itch. Ever since his friend Hickok took a bullet in the back in Deadwood, he'd had that little spot in his back that would itch once in a while.

"Look," Romeo said, "I don't care if you believe me or not. I'm gonna keep on doin' my job."

"Which is keeping me alive?"

"For now," Romeo said.

"Romeo, let me ask you . . . did you recognize any of the men we killed?"

"My boss asked me the same thing," Stanton said. "Everything happened too fast, or too far away. I got out of there without ever seeing their faces. So, no, I didn't."

"What's your best guess about who they worked for?"

"My best guess is Brockton."

"Mike Brockton."

"Right."

"I guess I should go talk to him."

"If you do that," Romeo said, "you might need more than me to keep you alive."

"Ah," Clint said, "it'll keep you on your toes. Finish your beer. I've got things to do."

"Are you goin' to see Brockton?"

"Eventually," Clint said, lowering his own mug after draining it, "but I've got somebody else to see first."

Clint turned and left. Romeo saw that Eddie had been listening to the conversation, so he jerked his thumb toward Steelgrave's office and then followed Clint out the door.

THIRTY-SIX

Now that Jane Hutchinson was dead, and it appeared she had set Clint up to be killed—and had tried to shoot him in the back—it made everything she'd told him or given him—especially names and addresses—suspect. So Clint decided to go and talk to the only person whose information he could trust.

He went back to the jail. . . .

"I can't believe it," Roper said. "You know, when Pitt told me, I thought he was just trying to trick me."

"Into what?"

"I don't know," Roper said. "I just never believe anything he says to me."

Talbot Roper looked tired and haggard. He also looked totally confused, which was an expression Clint had never seen on his friend's face before.

"Tal, I need help."

"That makes two of us."

Clint sat opposite him.

"I can't trust anything Hutch told me," Clint said. "This pretty much leaves me in the dark."

"Hutch," Roper said, shaking his head. "I still can't believe it."

"Face it," Clint said, "she took both of us in."

"Yeah," Roper said, "but she went to bed with you."

"And tried to shoot me in the back."

"At least you're still walking around free," Roper said.

"Okay," Clint said, "you win."

"I still can't believe she took me in," Roper said.

"Roper," Clint said, "give me somebody to talk to."

"The files are the files, Clint," Roper said. "Talk to the people in them."

"Before Hutch was killed," Clint said, "she gave me a new name out of one of the files. Somebody whose name wasn't in the copy she gave me."

"Which file?"

"Steelgrave's," Clint said. "This name was in it as an associate of Mike Brockton's."

"And whose name was it?"

Clint leaned forward and lowered his voice.

"Wilson Perry."

Romeo Stanton was uncomfortable standing outside the jail, so he went into a small saloon across the street, got a beer, and sat by the front window. Before he knew it, there were prison guards and policemen sitting around him, drinking. Without realizing it, he had taken refuge in a saloon that catered to the law.

He was wondering how to get out of the place without attracting attention.

"My Wilson Perry?" Roper asked.

"That's right."

"Can't be."

"Why not?"

"Well, first of all, I put those files together," Roper said, "and I didn't put Wilson in any of them. And second of all . . . well, there is no second of all. That's it."

"So she planted the name on me to make me suspect him?" Clint asked.

"Obviously."

"Perry has no connection with Mike Brockton?"

"Not that I know of," Roper said, "unless he represented him at some point . . . and what would be wrong with that?"

"I don't know," Clint said, "but I guess I better talk to your lawyer next after all."

Romeo saw Clint Adams come out the front of the jail and stop. The Gunsmith looked around, maybe trying to locate him. He knew he had to get out of the saloon now or lose Adams.

Slowly, he stood up, buttoned his jacket so none of the policemen or guards would see his gun, and walked out the front door. In the future, he'd have to watch what saloons he walked into.

Clint stopped just outside the door of the jail. He looked both ways and then across the street, but couldn't see Romeo Stanton. The man must be better at his job than Ted Lanigan had been.

He decided to leave Romeo to his own business. He had to go and find Wilson Perry. Roper had told him not to bother with Perry's office. The man would be in court at this time of the day. He told him to just get a cab and tell the driver to take him to the area of town where all the court buildings were.

"There's more than one?" he'd asked.

"It's a big city, Clint," Roper had replied. "There's a lot of crime."

Clint figured that, especially in his present situation, that was something Roper would know.

THIRTY-SEVEN

Clint saw Romeo Stanton when he got to the front door of the courthouse. The big man was standing across the street in plain sight this time. They looked at each briefly, and then Clint turned and went inside.

It took him a half an hour of hitting different court-rooms, but he finally located Perry. He was standing before a judge, arguing a case. Clint decided to wait outside rather than go inside and listen. The case meant nothing to him anyway.

"Adams."

He turned at the sound of his name. It was Lieutenant Pitt. The man looked down at Clint's hip, where the Navy Colt was resting in the borrowed holster, but for some reason the detective said nothing.

"What are you doing here?"

"Waiting for Wilson Perry."

"You two going to put your heads together again? Come up with a way to save Roper?"

"The only way to save him is to prove his innocence," Clint said. "That's what I intend to do."

"I wish I could wish you luck," Pitt said, "but I can't—no, actually, I won't."

With that Pitt walked away, but Clint didn't really notice. He realized something. There was someone he hadn't concentrated on at all, and he felt like a fool now that he realized it. He thought of leaving without talking to Perry but decided to stick it out now that he was there.

There was a bench in the hall, right next to the door of the courtroom, so he sat down to wait.

It took another half an hour, but finally the doors opened and people began filing out. Clint remained seated so he wouldn't be caught in the flow, then stood up when he saw Wilson Perry coming out.

"Perry!"

The lawyer looked around, saw Clint, and came over to him.

"You got something for me?"

"Have a seat here with me."

"I've got another case in"—he checked his watch—"ten minutes."

"That's enough time."

Perry sat down next to Clint.

"What's going on?"

"Let me fill you in."

He told the lawyer about what had happened with Jane Hutchinson.

"You must be on the right track if someone wants you dead that badly," the lawyer said. "We're getting somewhere."

"That's one way to look at it."

"Who was the man who helped you?"

"His name is Romeo Stanton. He works for Steelgrave."

"Steelgrave helped you?"

"He wants Roper to be proven innocent," Clint said.

"Well, that's good," Perry said.

"Wilson, I've got to ask you something."

"What?"

"Have you had any business dealings with Mike Brockton?"

"Why do you ask that?"

Clint told him about Jane Hutchinson's claim that his name was in the Steelgrave file as an associate of Brockton's.

"So?" Perry hesitated.

"Wilson?"

"I did some work for him when he first came to town," Perry finally said. "When I found out what he was really up to, though, I stopped working for him. If that makes me an associate . . ."

"It makes you a past associate," Clint said. "That's no so bad."

"Maybe not . . . anything else?"

"Just something that occurred to me a little while ago," Clint said. "The dead woman."

"Gloria Monahan."

"I just realized I haven't talked to anyone who knew her," Clint said, "anybody in her family."

"Why not, for Chrissake?"

"Maybe because people have been trying to kill me," Clint said testily. "Maybe because I'm not a damned detective."

"Okay, okay," Perry said. "Take it easy. If you haven't done it yet, then do it now."

"That's what I intend to do," Clint said, "but I need the address of her family."

They both stood up. Perry dug around in his leather case and came out with Roper's file. He looked up the address and wrote it on a scrap of paper for Clint.

"This next case is my last of the day," Perry said, "and

then I'll be working late in my office. You'll be able to find me there."

"Okay."

"Watch your back," Perry said. "We don't want to lose you."

"I've got Romeo doing that for me," Clint said.

"Don't trust him," the lawyer said. "If he works for Steelgrave . . . well, just don't trust him."

"I usually only trust myself, Wilson," Clint said.

Perry looked thoughtful.

"What is it?"

"I was wondering who else you could trust."

"There are a few men," Clint said, "but it would take a while to get them here."

"Nobody here in town?"

Clint started to say no, then checked himself and said, "Well, maybe one."

"Get him," Perry said. "We'll pay him too."

"I'll look into it," Clint said.

"Okay," Perry said. "See you later."

Clint nodded. The hall was remarkably empty now. He went one way, and the lawyer went the other.

Romeo saw Clint Adams come back outside. He scanned the street with his eyes, checked the rooftops. Everything looked clean. Adams looked across the street at him, and he nodded and waved that the street was all clear.

Clint walked down to the street, then waved Romeo over. The man crossed and joined him.

"We might as well take the same cab," he said. "We're going to the same place."

"And where's that?"

"Here." Clint showed him the address.

"Okay," Romeo said. "I know where this is."

They waited for a cab to come by. When one did, it stopped by itself to let somebody off, and they grabbed it and gave the driver the address.

THIRTY-EIGHT

The cab let Clint and Romeo off in front of a house in an expensive, residential section of Denver. The home they stood in front of was huge, almost like a government building.

"This is someone's house?" Romeo asked.

"Somebody with a lot of money to spend," Clint said.

"Or waste." Romeo seemed actually offended by the size of the house.

"You can wait out here if you like."

"I think I will," Romeo said. "If I go in, I might do or say something embarrassing."

"I shouldn't be long," Clint said. "I don't even know who I'm looking to talk to."

"Take your time. I'll be over there by that tree."

Romeo walked away, and Clint made his way up the front walk to the door and knocked. He waited a few moments because it was a big house, but then knocked again.

Finally, someone answered the door, a man in a dark suit and white shirt.

"Yes? Can I help you?"

"I'm looking for . . ." Clint didn't know who he was

looking for. "Someone who was related to Gloria Mona-han? Would that be you?"

"Hardly," the man said. "I am the butler, sir."

"She did live here, didn't she?"

"Yes."

"With, uh, who?"

"With Mr. Monahan, sir," the butler said. "He was her husband."

"Ah," Clint said, "okay, is Mr. Monahan home?"

"Who shall I say is calling?"

"My name is Clint Adams."

"And what may I say is your business, sir?"

Clint stared at the man for a few seconds, then said, "Gloria Monahan."

"Very good, sir," the butler said. "Wait here, please."

Before Clint could say anything else, the man closed the door in his face. Clint turned and looked over at Romeo Stanton, who was leaning against a tree, eyeing the street.

Before long, the door opened again and the butler said, "Follow me, please."

Clint had been in some large homes in the past but nothing like this. The entry hall alone was larger than most houses, and it seemed to take forever to cross it.

Clint expected to be shown to an office or den or sitting room or something like that, so he was surprised to be shown to the house's kitchen.

"Mr. Clint Adams, sir."

"Thank you, Clarence. That's all."

The tall, slender man, with remarkably long fingers and gray hair that came to a widow's peak, looked up as Clint entered and said, "I hope you don't mind talking while I cook."

"Not at all."

Not only were his fingers long, but they moved very quickly. He was doing something with a knife and a piece of meat that was yielding smaller and smaller pieces, and yet Clint could hardly follow. He was also wearing an apron over a shirt, vest, and tie.

"I'm Patrick Monahan," the man said. "You wanted to speak to me about my wife?"

"Yes," Clint said. "I'm working for Wilson Perry, who is—"

"—the attorney for Talbot Roper, the man accused of killing my wife. I know."

"Accused of killing your wife?"

"Well, I don't think he did it," Monahan said. "Do you?"

"Uh, no, but—"

"You're surprised that I feel that way?"

"Yes, I am."

"Don't be," Monahan said. "You see, I made a hideous mistake when I married my wife, Mr. Adams. I am—or was—some twenty-five years older than my wife. I did not think that would be a problem when we married, but I was wrong. She began running around with younger men, unsavory types at best, and she was spending my money on them at an alarming rate."

"Why didn't you divorce her?"

Monahan finished with his meat, put the knife down, began wiping his hands on a towel, and looked directly at Clint.

"Because to tell you the truth," he said, "I was convinced that, eventually, one of them would kill her."

"And that's what you think happened?"

"Yes."

"And did you tell that to the police?"

"Yes, I did," Monahan said. "I spoke to a lieutenant . . . Pitt, I think it was?"

"Yes," Clint said, "it probably was."

"He didn't think much of my opinion, though," the man said. "Seems he felt he had enough evidence against Mr. Roper."

"Mr. Monahan, do you know Talbot Roper?"

"Never met him."

"Did your wife know him?"

"Is Mr. Roper younger than I am?"

"I believe he might be. . . ."

"Then she probably knew him," Monahan said. "I can't say for sure, though. Gloria was in her mid-thirties when she was killed, and was still a remarkable beauty. She liked men her own age or younger, though."

"Mr. Monahan, if you'll forgive me for asking, you don't sound as if you hated your wife, or even disliked her."

"Why would I hate her?" Monahan asked. "She was only doing what came naturally to her. She loved sex, and I must say, on the occasional evening when she deemed me worthy of her body, I quite enjoyed it too. She was very skillful."

Clint had not heard many men discuss sex with their wives with another man.

"Do you know Wilson Perry?" he asked.

"Yes," Monahan said. "Most of the wealthy men in this city know Wilson, I think. He's quite a good lawyer. I hope he manages to get Mr. Roper off. Excuse me, I have to heat a pan."

He turned to the stove, dropped some butter into a frying pan, and then put it over a low flame.

"Cooking is my passion, Mr. Adams," he said with his back turned. "I suppose if sex had been my passion, I would have resented Gloria a lot more."

"But you did resent her?"

Monahan half-turned and looked at Clint over his shoulder.

"I suppose I did, from time to time," he said, and then turned back to the pan. "I'm preparing a meal for one, sir, but it could just as easily be two. Would you care to join me?"

"No," Clint said, "but thank you for the offer."

The man turned completely around this time to look at Clint.

"Is there anything else I can tell you?"

"I don't know, Mr. Monahan," Clint said. "Is there? Can you give me a name?"

"A name?"

"A man who, maybe, you think finally killed your wife?"

Monahan thought for a few moments, then said, "She used to go down to the docks a lot."

"The docks?"

"I suppose she was . . . trolling, would you call it?"

"Where on the docks?"

Monahan raised a finger to Clint to signal him to wait, and called out, "Clarence!"

The butler appeared in three seconds flat, leading Clint to believe that he was nearby, listening in.

"Sir?"

"Where on the docks did my wife go to look for her men?" Monahan asked.

"I believe the place was called the River's Edge, sir."

"The River's Edge? Are you sure?" Clint asked.

"Quite sure, sir."

"Thank you, Clarence."

"Yes, sir."

Clarence backed out of the room, but Clint was willing to bet he wouldn't go too far. He had just noticed that Clarence the butler was wearing a gun under his left arm. It probably meant that Clarence the butler was much more than just that.

"Does that help you at all?" Monahan asked.

"Actually, it kind of confuses things."

Monahan made a sympathetic face that didn't last long.

"I really have to get back to my meal, Mr. Adams," he said. "One last question?"

Clint groped for one as Monahan began taking his strips of meat and dropping them into the frying pan, where they began to sizzle.

"Okay, then," Clint said. "Point me toward the last man you heard your wife was seeing."

"You know," Monahan said, "I offered to do that for the lieutenant, but he declined my help."

"Well, I'll take it."

Monahan took a moment to think, then said, "I think the name was Brock."

"Brockton?" Clint offered.

"That was it!" Monahan said triumphantly. "Mike Brockton."

THIRTY-NINE

Clint left the home of Patrick Monahan more confused than ever. If the man—and his butler—were to be believed, Gloria Monahan had ties to Mike Brockton and to Harvey Steelgrave, via his saloon, the River's Edge. Well, at least he had some contacts with that saloon.

"You look confused," Romeo said when Clint walked over and joined him by his tree.

"I am," Clint said. "Romeo, do you know what Gloria Monahan looked like?"

"Sure," the man said. "Everyone in town did. She was a good-looking woman."

"And how often did she show up at the River's Edge?"

"From time to time."

"And would she leave with a man?"

"Every time."

"She ever leave with Steelgrave?"

"No," Romeo said. "The boss wouldn't touch her."

"How did he treat her?"

"Like a guest in his house."

"Did she ever leave with anyone you know?"

"Sure," Romeo said. "She's been with Johnny, Bill, Wade, Carlos, Zeke. . . ."

"Eddie?"

"No, not that I know of."

"What about you?"

"Me?" Clint wondered if the man would get insulted, but he simply looked baffled. "No, not me. Why me?"

"I was just asking."

"She came down there to go slumming," Romeo said. "She was looking for river rats, and that's what she got."

"And so maybe one of those river rats killed her?"

"Probably."

"You mean you don't think Roper did it either?"

"I don't know him," Romeo said, "but I think it's more likely she went off with the wrong guy."

"Then how did she end up in the building where she was found?" Clint asked.

"I don't know anything about that," Romeo said. "I don't know where she was found."

"Okay, what about this?" Clint asked. "Monahan says he thinks his wife was with Mike Brockton recently."

"That don't figure."

"Why not?"

"He's a boss, like Mr. Steelgrave," Romeo said. "Not a river rat."

"Mike Brockton wouldn't be slumming for someone like Gloria Monahan?"

"It don't figure for me," Romeo Stanton said, "but then, I ain't a detective."

"Neither am I," Clint said. "That's part of the problem."

"So what do we do next?"

"I want to get a look at the building Gloria was found in," Clint said. "It's getting later, so we better go now, before it closes."

"We won't catch a cab here," Romeo said. "Let's walk a few blocks. It'll be easier."

"Lead the way."

∙   ∙   ∙

They walked several blocks until they came to a busier
street, one that was lined with businesses, and not homes.
Romeo waved a cab down, and then they got in.

"Where to?"

Clint didn't answer, but before long Romeo told the
driver where to take them.

FORTY

When the cab let them off in front of the building, Romeo said, "I'll wait out here, watch the street."

"I just want to have a look around," Clint said. "I'll be right out."

Romeo nodded and went off to find himself a comfortable place to wait and watch.

Clint went into the building. Just inside the door was the hole that Roper had fallen through. Boards had been placed over it so that the businesses in the building could continue. There was a directory in the lobby, and reading it, Clint saw that there were some lawyers with offices in the building. He didn't recognize any of the names.

He turned and looked down at the boarded-up hole again. The rest of the floor was not rotted, so Roper had not simply fallen through beneath his own weight. The trap had been set, and Gloria Monahan's name had been used to set it. But why? Roper didn't know her, had never met her before that night. Why choose to use her, unless it was a way to get rid of two people at one time?

Suddenly, something occurred to him. He'd heard it earlier, but it hadn't registered. And then he knew—or thought he did. Some of it anyway.

He went back outside and found Romeo Stanton was gone.

When Clint walked into the River's Edge, Romeo wasn't there. As usual, the other men in the place looked him over, but he was under the protection of Steelgrave there. It was for that reason that he chose to stop at the bar rather than simply burst into the man's office again.

"Eddie."

The bartender saw him and came down to his end of the bar. "Beer?"

"Did Romeo come back here today?"

"No," Eddie said. "I thought he was following you."

"So did I," Clint said. "Is Steelgrave in?"

"Yes."

"Ask him if he'll see me."

"All right."

Eddie went to his boss's office, then came out and waved at Clint to come.

"Not busting in on people anymore, Mr. Adams?" Steelgrave asked.

"You told me you'd help if you could."

"And I meant it."

"I found out who killed Gloria Monahan."

Steelgrave sat forward in his chair.

"That sounds interesting," he said. "Do I get to know?"

"I don't think you'll like the answer to that question."

"Ah," Steelgrave said, sitting back, "it's getting more interesting. Come on, don't keep me in suspense. Who killed her?"

Clint turned, closed the door behind him, then turned to face Steelgrave and said, "Romeo."

Romeo Stanton was across from the River's Edge when Clint Adams went inside. He'd realized his mistake just moments before Clint had, and so had left immediately.

He'd needed some time to decide what to do, because he didn't have time to check with his boss first.

Now that he had decided, he only needed to wait.

"Romeo?" Steelgrave asked. "That's ridiculous."

"Is it?"

"He didn't know her."

"He didn't have to," Clint said. "Somebody wanted her dead."

"Who?"

"The same person who wanted Roper out of the way," Clint said. "So they decided to get rid of them both at the same time."

"Kill her, frame him."

"Right."

"What makes you think it was Romeo?"

"We were talking earlier today, and he said he didn't know the building where Gloria was killed."

"So?"

"So I told him I wanted to see the building," Clint said. "We got into a cab, and he gave the driver the address."

"Ah . . ."

"It didn't dawn on me until I went inside," Clint said. "When I came out, he was gone."

"He would have realized it too."

"So I came back here."

"He's not here."

"I know."

"Oh, I see," Steelgrave said. "You think that because he works for me, I must be the one who gave him his orders."

"No," Clint said, "I don't think that."

"Why not?"

"Because I think you really do want Talbot Roper to be found innocent."

"So then who is he working for?"

"I think Romeo knew that Roper would eventually find

out that he wasn't really working for you. So he framed Roper for killing Gloria Monahan."

"Why not just kill him?"

Clint thought a moment, then said, "Maybe the idea wasn't his. Maybe it came from whoever he's working for, and that person had a reason to want to get rid of both of them."

"Confusing," Steelgrave said, "but somehow it makes sense."

"So the question is, who would want to put someone inside your circle?"

"Well," Steelgrave said, "there's only one answer to that question. Mike Brockton."

"And why would Brockton want Gloria dead?"

"I don't know that."

"Romeo told me she came down here trolling for men."

"On occasion."

"He said he thought one of them probably killed her. He also told me Mike Brockton would never have been with Gloria."

"But maybe he had."

"And maybe he didn't want her rich husband to know."

"But why not?" Steelgrave asked. "She'd been with so many men, why not one more?"

"Because maybe," Clint said, "this was the first man she'd ever been with who was doing business with her husband."

FORTY-ONE

Romeo Stanton kept his eyes on the front door of the River's Edge. Two of Mike Brockton's men were off to the right, and two to the left. They were watching Romeo, waiting for the word.

"So," Steelgrave said, "she slept with one of Monahan's business associates, and rather than kill him, Monahan kills her?"

Clint shrugged. "Wouldn't you call that good business?"

Steelgrave looked surprised. "As a matter of fact, I would. So he orders Romeo—but wait a minute. That means that Romeo is working for . . . for Monahan?"

"Romeo," Clint said, "is working all three ends against the middle."

"But who is he really working for?" Steelgrave asked. "Not me certainly."

"Maybe he killed Gloria for her husband and framed Roper to keep from being exposed as a spy in your camp."

"A double spy."

"Maybe triple."

"Sonofabitch," Steelgrave said. "I hate being played for a fool."

He got up from his desk, walked to the door, opened it, and shouted, "Eddie!"

He went back to his desk. Eddie appeared in the doorway.

"Yeah, Boss?"

"It's my guess that Romeo is waiting outside for Mr. Adams," Steelgrave said. "It's also my guess he's not alone. Confirm that for me."

"Okay, Boss."

"And don't make a mistake," Steelgrave said. "I don't want to get killed because you can't count."

"Right, Boss."

As Eddie left, Steelgrave turned to his gun cabinet, opened it, and took out a rolled-up holster.

"*You* don't want to die?" Clint asked.

Steelgrave, strapping on his gun, turned to face Clint.

"I'm not gonna let you go out there alone," he said, shifting the holster until it was comfortable. "You revealed a spy in my world. I owe you for that."

"You don't owe me—"

"Then I owe Romeo," Steelgrave said, "and whoever hired him."

"You got any more men out there?"

"Eddie," Steelgrave said, "but he's just a bartender."

"What about all those other men?"

"Customers," he said. "River rats. I have more men, but I'd never get them here in time. It's just you and me."

Eddie reappeared in the doorway.

"How many?" Steelgrave asked.

"Five," Eddie said, "including Romeo. He's right across the way. Then there are two to the right, two to the left."

"You recognize any of them?"

"No, Boss."

"Okay, go back behind the bar."

"Boss," Eddie said, "I got my shotgun—"

"Back behind the bar, Eddie."

"Yes, Boss."

Steelgrave looked at Clint. "I believe if any of the men outside worked for Brockton, Eddie would have recognized them."

"So you're saying they work for Patrick Monahan?"

"Or someone else."

"Like who?"

"I don't know," Steelgrave said. "An unknown player."

"We don't need any unknown players."

"Why don't we just deal with what's outside?" Steelgrave suggested. "I'm looking forward to seeing you in action."

"You any good with that thing?" Clint asked, indicating the gun on Steelgrave's hip.

"I guess we're gonna find out."

FORTY-TWO

Clint and Steelgrave walked through the River's Edge to the front door. Every man in the place knew what was going to happen, but none of them moved until the two men had gone out the front door. Then the place erupted as they all left their seats and ran to the windows to watch.

Romeo was surprised to see Clint Adams come out the front door with Harvey Steelgrave. It didn't matter, though. He would have taken five-to-two odds any day. He looked to the left, then to the right, before stepping out into the street.

As Clint and Steelgrave stepped out, Clint said, "You take the two on the left. I'll take the two on the right."

"What about Romeo?"

"I'll take him."

"He should be mine," Steelgrave said.

"Tell you what," Clint said. "He's the one we've got to take first. Why not leave him to me? I'm hoping we won't have to kill him."

"Why?"

"We need him to clear Roper."

173

"All right," Steelgrave said, "You take him."

At that moment, Romeo stepped into the street across from them. Both of them also stepped into the street.

"What are you doing, Boss?" Romeo asked.

"Don't 'Boss' me, you traitor," Steelgrave shouted.

Romeo looked at Clint then and said, "It was the address, wasn't it?"

"That's right," Clint said. "How'd you know the address after you told me you didn't know where Gloria was killed?"

"I have a big mouth sometimes. I was hoping it would just be you and me, Adams. One on one. I'd like to try myself against the great Gunsmith."

"And what about the other four men?" Steelgrave asked. "Are they just gonna watch?"

Romeo firmed his jaw.

"Fuck it," he said, and went for his gun.

At the same moment, his men stepped into the street and grabbed for theirs.

Clint drew first. He hated trying trick shots, but he needed Romeo alive. His first shot hit the big man in the right shoulder, numbing his arm and hand. He dropped his gun to the ground, but stooped immediately to pick it up left-handed.

Clint turned his attention to the two men on his right. He drilled one of them through the chest before he had a chance to clear leather. The other man actually got his gun out, but he never got to point it. A bullet hit him in the throat and he fell onto his face.

On the right Steelgrave drew his gun. He was not as fast as Clint, so he was going to have to count on accuracy. His two men got their guns out and brought them up. Steelgrave's first shot hit one of them in the face, but the other managed to get off a shot. Steelgrave felt the bullet punch a hole in his jacket and go on through, missing him completely. Before the man had time to pull the trigger again, Steelgrave shot him in the belly.

Both Clint and Steelgrave turned their attention back to Romeo as the man snatched his gun from the ground left-handed and brought it up.

"No!" Clint shouted.

He held his fire, but Steelgrave calmly shot Romeo in the chest.

"Damn it," Clint said.

"He's as good left-handed as right-handed," Steelgrave said. "You didn't know that."

"No," Clint said, "I didn't."

They walked to Romeo and stared down at his still form. Clint kicked his gun away from him, then dropped to one knee and turned him over, hoping to find him alive. Instead, he found Romeo's dead eyes staring up at him.

"I'm sorry," Steelgrave said. "It was . . . reflex. I'm . . . sorry."

"Don't be sorry," Clint said. "You did the right thing."

Eddie came up behind them and announced, "The others are all dead, Boss."

"Thanks, Eddie."

The bartender turned to Clint and said, "I ain't never seen anybody draw so fast."

Clint simply nodded.

"What now?" Steelgrave asked. "Have I killed Roper's chance to get out of jail?"

"Maybe not," Clint said. He looked at Eddie. "Still don't recognize any of the others as Brockton's men?"

"No."

"So that makes it Patrick Monahan Romeo was working for," Clint said. "He probably used Monahan's money to hire them."

"So Brockton's out of the running?"

"For now," Clint said. "He had Lanigan watching me, but that was probably just to keep tabs on me while I was in Denver. Maybe he thought you had brought me in to take care of him."

Steelgrave slapped his forehead and said, "Why didn't I think of that?"

FORTY-THREE

When the butler opened the door this time, Clint punched him in the face, then stepped in and disarmed him before he could regain his balance. He pointed the man's own gun at him.

"Where's your boss? In the kitchen again? Still?"

Clarence didn't answer. He stared at Clint calmly.

"Okay, let's go look. Lead the way."

When the man didn't move, Clint turned him around forcefully and shoved him ahead of him. They walked that way to the kitchen, where Patrick Monahan seemed to be in the act of making a pie.

"Mr. Adams," he said. "To what do I owe—"

"Cut the crap, Monahan," Clint said. He shoved the butler over next to his boss. "Romeo is dead."

"Romeo?"

"Dead, but he talked first. He told me and Steelgrave that he was working for you. That he killed Gloria and framed Roper."

"He framed Roper? How amusing."

"So you admit he killed your wife for you?"

"You say he killed my wife," Monahan replied. "I take

your word for that. And framing Roper? Again, if you say so. I admit nothing."

Clint cocked the hammer on the butler's short-barreled, nickel-plated Colt.

"You won't shoot me," Monahan said. "If you think I can clear Roper, you won't kill me."

"And can you clear him?"

"I might be able to."

"Will you?"

"Put the gun down—"

"Would you clear him if you could?"

"No."

"Then I've got nothing to lose by killing you."

Clint pointed the gun and Monahan yelled, "All right, stop!"

"Make it quick."

"Suppose I give you Clarence," Monahan said.

"What?" Clarence said.

"I'll say Clarence did it, which will clear your friend . . . and I'll pay you ten thousand dollars."

"I don't want Clarence," Clint said. "I want you."

Clint saw Monahan's eye go to the knife on the counter in front of him.

"You know," the rich man said, "my kitchen knives are perfectly balanced—"

"Don't even think about it, Monahan."

"Clarence?"

It was clear Monahan wanted Clarence to go for the knife and use it on Clint.

"Go for it yourself," Clarence said. "I'm through." He looked at Clint. "He did it. He had her killed. He—"

Monahan went for the knife and as Clint shot him, he stabbed Clarence in the stomach with it. The rich man staggered back, a look of surprise and shock on his face. He couldn't buy his way out of this one. He staggered, went to his knees, and died. He didn't feel a thing when his face hit the floor.

Clint hurried to the butler, who was on his knees, holding his stomach. The butcher knife was sticking out of his belly, and blood was streaming down.

"Clarence—"

"He did it," the man gasped. "Was going to sacrifice me after . . . after years of service . . ." Suddenly, a great gout of blood came from his mouth, and he shuddered and died. Clint caught him and gently laid him on the floor.

"Damn it," he said. "Tell me you're out there, Pitt, and you heard all of this."

There was no answer.

"Ah, goddamn—" Clint began but stopped when Pitt stepped into the room.

"I didn't hear it all," the policeman said, "but I heard enough."

EPILOGUE

Roper and Clint were having breakfast together in the Denver House dining room three days later. The detective had been released the day before, had gotten himself a bath, a shave, and a haircut, and was now buying Clint breakfast as partial thanks for getting him out.

"I'm surprised Pitt listened to Steelgrave and even went to Patrick Monahan's house," Roper said.

"Why else would a man like Steelgrave go to him if it wasn't for good reason?" Clint asked. "In the end, Pitt was an honest policeman who wanted the real killer."

"And you handed them to him," Roper said, "dead. He couldn't have been too happy about that."

"He wasn't," Clint said, "but you're out."

"Yes," Roper said, "I'm out, and this breakfast is poor thanks."

"You have to thank Steelgrave too," Clint said.

"I will," Roper said, "but you found the traitor in his midst, so you took care of that job for me." And, Clint thought, Tom Horn is taking care of the rancher's job.

"You still have the banker waiting for you to solve his problem," Clint said.

"And I will," Roper said, "As soon as I get the smell of a jail cell out of my nose."

They ate some more, had some coffee, and then Roper sat back.

"I still can't believe it about Hutch," he said.

"Maybe there's nothing to believe, Tal."

"What do you mean?"

"Well, Romeo turned out to be the bad guy," Clint said. "Maybe he killed Hutch because she was going to use her gun on him."

"Hey, that's right," Roper said. "Why should we believe anything he said? I think you're right, Clint. At least, I choose to think you're right."

"I found out something else for you," Clint said. "In fact, it was Wilson who found it out."

"What's that?"

"Monahan had no ties to the Wyoming Stock Growers' Association, so they probably had no hand in any of this at all."

"That's good to know," Roper said. "I've done some work for them in the past. They pay well."

"Wouldn't want you to lose a good-paying customer."

They paid their bill and left the dining room to go out into the lobby. Clint had paid for his room and had a train to catch.

"I can take you to the station," Roper said.

"Shake hands with me here and go get your life in order, Tal."

Rather than shake hands, Roper embraced Clint, squeezing him tightly enough to force the air from his lungs.

"Thanks, Clint," he said. "Thanks a lot."

Clint watched Roper leave the hotel, then heard a woman ask behind him, "Leaving us?"

He turned to find Elizabeth Hannibal standing there.

"Yes, I am," Clint said. "I'm done here."

"Things turned out as you hoped?"

"Better."

"I'm glad," she said. "Listen, I'm sorry about what happened—"

"Don't be," he said. "I'm not."

She stared at him, then nodded.

"Come and see us again," she said.

"I will," he said.

"Maybe," she said, "we can spend some time together . . . away from the hotel."

He smiled and said, "I'd like that a lot."

Watch for

THE RECKONING

280th novel in the exciting GUNSMITH
series from Jove

Coming in April!

J. R. ROBERTS

THE GUNSMITH

Explore the exciting Old West with one of the men who made it wild!

AVAILABLE WHEREVER BOOKS ARE SOLD OR AT
WWW.PENGUIN.COM

(Ad # B112)

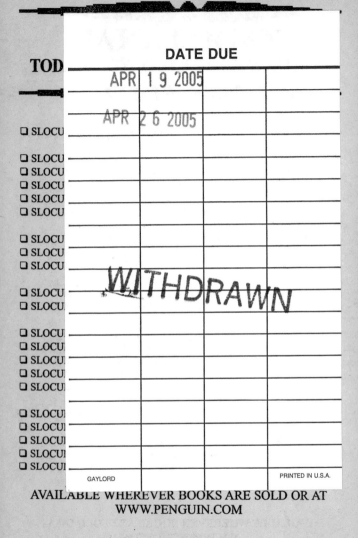

TOD

❏ SLOCU

❏ SLOCU
❏ SLOCU
❏ SLOCU
❏ SLOCU
❏ SLOCU

❏ SLOCU
❏ SLOCU
❏ SLOCU

❏ SLOCU
❏ SLOCU

❏ SLOCU
❏ SLOCU
❏ SLOCU
❏ SLOCU
❏ SLOCU

❏ SLOCU
❏ SLOCU
❏ SLOCU
❏ SLOCU
❏ SLOCU